THE STUBBORN LORD

DRAGON LORDS: A QURILIXEN WORLD NOVEL

MICHELLE M. PILLOW

MICHELLE M. PILLOW® - MICHELLEPILLOW.COM

ABOUT THE STUBBORN LORD

DRAGON LORDS 6

Dragon-shifter Romance
by Michelle M. Pillow

Repossessed…

Kendall Haven's life turns upside down when she's kidnapped off her fueling dock home by thugs claiming to have the right. Her father, the gambler, used her to cover his losses at the Larceny Casino Ship. Drugged and treated like cargo, she's sold to the highest bidder— Galaxy Brides Corporation.

Landing on a primitive planet on the far edge of the universe, she has no intention of fulfilling her father's contract—even if that contract includes marriage to a very handsome, very sexy, very intense barbarian of a man. He might be everything a woman fantasizes about, but he wants a little more than she can give.

Possession…

Lord Alek, Younger Duke of Draig, has not been lucky in finding his life mate. Resigned to a lonely life, he attends the bridal ceremony out of familial duty. Then the impossible happens—Kendall. Nothing goes according to tradition, but he can't let that dissuade him. She is his only chance at happiness, and no matter how she protests, he's not going to let her get away.

NEW TO DRAGON LORDS?

Dragon Lords books 1-8 follow a concurrent time line. The fun of this is that the events you read in one book might be examined from a different point of view, sometimes with overlapping or expanded scenes, sometimes with events you might have wondered about in another book. You might even discover secrets as characters interact with each other. I recommend reading them in order to get the full effect. However if you bought the books out of order, no worries, each book is technically a standalone story for the hero and heroine.

DRAGON LORDS SERIES

PART OF THE QURILIXEN WORLD
COLLECTION

Dragon Lords Books 1 - 4

The dragon-shifting princes have no problem with commitment. In one night, they will meet and choose their life mate in a simplistic ceremony involving the removing of masks and the crushing of crystals. With very few words spoken and the shortest, most bizarre courtship in history, they will bond to their women forever. And once bonded, these men don't let go...

Too bad nobody explained this to their brides.

Dragon Lords Books 5-8

The noblemen brothers aren't new to the sacred Qurilixian bridal ceremony. After several failed attempts at finding a bride, it's hard to get excited about yet another festival. No matter how honorably they try to live, it would seem fate thinks them unworthy of such happiness—that is until now.

With very few words spoken and the shortest, most bizarre courtship in history, they will bond to their women forever. And once bonded, these men don't let go...

Too bad nobody explained this to their brides.

Dragon Lords Book 9

Before four princes and four noblemen found their brides, before the death of the Var King Attor and the threat of the Tyoe miners, there was a time of peace on the planet of Qurilixen. It was not a strong peace, but it had lasted for quite some time between the cat-shifting Var kingdom and their northern neighbors the dragon-shifting Draig. It lasted because both sides had very little to do with each other.

This was the time before the great war came to rift the planet apart—dragon against cat. The only battles were skirmishes along the borderlands over territory and drunken brawls that erupted to prove which shifter side was of superior strength. It is here the dragons found their queen.

Spin-off Series

Dragon Lords is the first installment in the multiple bestselling romance series. As of this publication, there are nine Dragon Lords books.

The series continues with the *Lords of the Var®* series, Space Lords series, Dynasty Lords Series, Captured by a Dragon-Shifter series, Galaxy Alien Mail Order Brides series, and Qurilixen Lords series.

There will be more books and more series to come. They can be read alone, but the author recommends reading books in order of release.

For details please visit www.michellepillow.com

The Playful Prince
The Bound Prince
The Rogue Prince
The Pirate Prince

Captured by a Dragon-Shifter Series
Determined Prince
Rebellious Prince
Stranded with the Cajun
Hunted by the Dragon
Mischievous Prince
Headstrong Prince

Space Lords Series
His Frost Maiden
His Fire Maiden
His Metal Maiden
His Earth Maiden
His Woodland Maiden

Dynasty Lords Series

Seduction of the Phoenix

Temptation of the Butterfly

To learn more about the Qurilixen World series of
books and to stay up to date on the latest book list
visit www.MichellePillow.com

To the fabulous editor extraordinaire Heidi Moore, Dianne B the final line editor, Natalie Winters the cover artist, and all the other wonderful people who helped this book see publication. As always, to my readers: You're the best!

And to acknowledge the hard work of Rocky the Cat who made the following addition into the book during edits: qwwwwwwwwwwwwwwwwwwwwwwwwwwwwwwwwwwwwwwwwwwwww-wwwwwwwwwwwwwwwwwwwwwwwwwwwwwwwwwwwwww2222222 We love you, Rocky.

X QUADRANT ROAMING FUELING STATION

Registered Deep Space Port X-65J

"Let me free!" Kendall Haven kicked her legs, violently trying to loosen herself from the grasp of her would-be kidnappers. Though they lifted her off the ground, she'd managed to wedge her feet and hands against the metal door frame to her office. They had tried to heft her into the corridor head first.

"What do you think you are doing? There are security cameras all over this vessel. You won't get away with this."

It was a lie. The security cameras were nonfunctional and she'd been unable to fix them. Well, saying they were nonfunctional was just a polite way of describing what had really happened.

Her father had lost a key part to the circuitry to some traveling casino workers in a game of chance.

"Sorry, Girl One Haven, this is a legally sanctioned repossession," said the man struggling with her feet. "If you stop resisting, we will set you down and let you walk."

"Repossession? I'm not a blasted spaceship." She kicked harder. The fact that the two men wore dingy-gray salvage uniforms didn't help calm her fears. "I owe no debts!" Then, seeing her father's pale face in the corridor, hope filled her. He wouldn't let these crazy men attack her.

The fueling dock was her home. She'd never lived anywhere else. The large ship circled the X quadrant at regular intervals to service nearby planets when not stationed at Deep Space Port X in docking lot 65J. Even docked, she rarely left the vessel unless it was to check fuel hoses or work the occasional fueling shift when a worker skipped out on his job. The space port was nothing more than a giant docking lot filled with a variety of ships. Travelers came to her home vessel for food, lodging and fuel. That was the extent of her socializing. This was all she knew.

"You are now casino property," the man at her head explained.

Her father swayed lightly and blinked his liquor-addled eyes as he mumbled, "I'm sorry. I'm sorry. Forgive me. I'm sorry. I thought I could win you back. It was such a good hand. I shouldn't have been able to lose. At least I didn't give them Margot. She's too young. You would have told me your sister is too young."

For a moment, Kendall froze in shock, and the two men were able to carry her through the doorway into the corridor. As they neared her father, the man at her feet reached into his pocket to hand him a slip of paper. "Here is a copy of your receipt, Debtor Haven, don't lose it. There is no electronic copy. Thank you for turning her over. The casino will resell the property and you are liable for any remaining debt. If the property sells for more than the debt, you will be issued space credits at the Larceny Casino Ship in the extra amount minus a processing fee. This does include the virtual gaming tables if you cannot make it onboard the ship."

Her father actually seemed to smile for the briefest of moments as he took the paper in his shaking hands.

She didn't think, merely acted out of fear. Taking advantage of the man's distraction, Kendall kicked. She somehow managed to free herself from the repossession workers' grasps by twisting and jerking. Her hip hit the metal floor first and she pushed up, half-running, half-limping toward freedom. She didn't know where she was going, or how she would get off this floating space dock, but right now that didn't matter. She would find a place to hide until she could grab Margot and get out of here. Or until she could figure out just how much money her father had lost. There were still things of value on the ship, things she'd hidden from her father, things she didn't want to sell but could.

One of the men growled in frustration. The sound of their footfalls never reverberated behind her. They didn't give chase. When she neared the platform grate that would take her down a level, she glanced back. She saw the blast of a tazer seconds before feeling the jolt of electricity inside her body, burning its way down to her feet. Her lips parted to scream and she began to pitch forward. She saw the metal steps coming toward her but couldn't make her limbs move to block the fall as the world went black.

SOMETIME LATER...

Bright lights flashed against Kendall's eyelids, jerking her brain to consciousness. Her skin tingled with a familiar sensation, but she couldn't readily determine the cause of the feeling. Streaks of warmth snaked across her flesh, her naked flesh, *completely* naked flesh. Stiffening, she gasped as she opened her eyes. A barrier blocked her face and she lifted her hands in automatic defense. Her fingers struck the blockade, her hands as trapped as her head. When she bent her knees and kicked her feet, the same thing happened. Green lasers flashed and slid over her body. Awareness pierced her confusion. She was in a medic unit getting a health scan. What had happened? Why did she need a medic? It must have been a serious accident for her father to have allowed for the expensive treatment.

Kendall started to call out for her father and little sister but stopped when she remembered what had happened. He'd turned her in to pay his gambling debts. So instead, she kept quiet and reached to the side, trying to find an opening to the unit. Her fingers found the cool of outside air and she wiggled them to feel around the small opening. The release latch wouldn't move. She was locked inside. Desperate, she called out, "Hayo?"

No one answered her hoarse greeting. Instead, a needle pierced her back. Heat released into her body before blackness consumed her once more.

Draig Northern Mountain Fortress, Planet of Qurilixen

Marriage was the last thing Lord Aleksej, Younger Duke of Draig, wanted to think about. He didn't want to take time out of his work to put on a fur loincloth, hide his face under a mask, only to stand in line looking at eligible females—women that would never be his. Like the preceding years, he would wait for the sacred crystal around his neck to glow to signify he'd found his true mate, all the while knowing it probably never would.

He had actually thought about it quite a bit. With all the planets and space stations in all the universes, what were the odds that his true mate would find her way here? What if her ship had crashed on her way to him, and he would never know about it? What if she'd died in a childhood accident? What if her lifespan had yet to start and he wouldn't find her until he was hundreds of years old and close to his own death? How could he be expected to believe his fifth attempt would turn out differently?

Oh, right. Fate. The will of the gods.

Alek used to believe in the will of the gods, but somewhere along the way his faith had wavered. How could it not? He lived honorably. Over the past four years he had gone to the bridal ceremony, hoping, praying, only to come home alone. He was ready for the pain to be over. He was ready to accept his fate of solitude and duty.

Alek did want a wife. He wanted one terribly. But the disappointment and loneliness had been hard lessons to live with. Just because he was willing did not mean he would find her. His older brother, Bron, the high duke, faced his seventh attempt. Mirek faced his fourth festival. The youngest of them, Vladan, prepared for his first. For some reason, the gods had not seen fit to bless any of the brothers with a life mate.

Glancing down at his neck where the dormant crystal hung from a leather strap, he frowned. Only when he saw his future bride would the crystal glow, an unmistakable sign of destined fates. Perhaps their crystals were tarnished, or broken. Then again, perhaps the gods did not think them worthy. No answer satisfied his honor. No amount of praying brought him answers.

"Lord Alek?"

Alek blinked in surprise and looked up from where he stared at the rounded belly of the pregnant ceffyl, stirred from his thoughts of the upcoming festival. The beast was nearing her time and it was his duty to make sure she made it to term. As Top Breeder, a very important position on his planet, his whole life focused around mares and steeds. His animals supplied the soldiers, helped the farmers, provided planetary travel and, in extreme times, meat. The animal opened its mouth, hissing as a long tongue slithered from between her lips. Ceffyls had the eyes of a reptile, the face and hooves of a beast of burden and the body of a small elephant. And, with a three-year gestation period and only about fifty percent live-birth rate, it was a resource that could not easily be replaced should something happen.

"She's close," he answered Cenek, one of his best trainers. "I hate to leave, but I cannot miss this festival. My cousins are attending for the first time, and I must go to support them. Let us hope the princes are more blessed than we. Prince Ualan, especially. As the future king, it is he who should find love first."

Cenek nodded, not commenting on the four princes's attendance. He had found his wife after one attempt, but then, he'd already met her before-hand at a space station where he'd escorted Mirek on an ambassadorial trip. For him, the ceremony had been a mere formality.

"She will be fine." Cenek reached out a callused hand to pet the pregnant animal. "I will sleep nearby and check on her hourly while you are gone. The Breeding Festival is only for one night. Perhaps this will be a blessed year and you will come home with a wife."

Alek stood, dusting off his hands. He had nothing to say to the words of encouragement, for he did not feel their truth and he refused to lie for the sake of politeness. He patted the beast a couple times before leaving the stables. As the fresh air hit him, he let himself wonder for the briefest of moments what a woman would think of his home. Surrounded by steep mountains, narrow passes and rocky crags dotted with lush plant life, the castle stood out against the elements like a timeless fortress. His mother, before her death, had loved the mountains. Sometimes, in the quietness of dusk as people settled into their homes, he imagined he could still hear her laughter ringing out over the valleys.

Unlike most other civilizations, the Draig chose to live simply. Even though they had the ability for deep-space travel, they normally only used it when ambassadorial duties demanded. Otherwise, they hid their technology in an elegant façade of stone and wood, choosing to do for themselves. Why have a food simulator materialize a meal when the earth could provide fresh vegetables and strong livestock? Why let machines serve when your own hands could do a better job? If they let technology do everything, society would become lazy. If that happened, an alien species would surely swoop in and take over the lucrative ore mines.

The castle nestled in the valley next to a jutting peak, a mere front for the homes hidden within the mountain's core. That was where Alek lived, as did his three brothers. Here the earth was red with streaks of gray through the stone. When they traveled south to the ceremony, near the Draig palace at the base of the mountains, the ground would become a dark red and the trees so large a home could fit comfortably within a single trunk.

Qurilixen had three suns—two yellow and one blue—and one moon, which made for a particularly bright planet. Female children were rare due to the blue radiation from those suns. Over the generations, it had altered the men's genetics to produce strong male warriors. Only once in a thousand births was a Qurilixian female born. In the old days, they had used portals to snatch foreign brides from their homes and bring them back to Qurilixen.

There were rumors that the Draig species had originated on the human planet Earth and actually traveled through some magical portal to capture women, but there was no proof that was true. Just as there was no actual proof that their dragon-shifter ancestors had actually flown when in shifted form.

The fact they had nearly no women of their own was why the services of corporations like Galaxy Brides were so invaluable to them now. In return for women willing to marry a stranger, the

Draig men would mine the rare ore found in their caves. Alek's family oversaw the mines, not Alek directly, but his brothers. The mines were a long-standing family duty. The last he'd heard reported from his brothers, there was a surplus of ore. That had to be a good omen. Perhaps this bridal ceremony would show a surplus of brides.

Who was he fooling? This year felt no different than the others. There would be no wife to show this place to, no woman in his bed, no heart to beat with his own. The hopelessness was perhaps the hardest part to face, coupled with the realization that he and his brothers were destined to be forever lonely. There had to be a reason none of them had found love, year after year, when so many others had.

Alek sighed, turning his attention from the towering castle to the large rectangular structure of the stables. He would do best to focus on his work. "A quick trip down and back. That's all this is. An ambassadorial trip to support my princely cousins, nothing else."

The sound of his own voice did little to comfort him, so he did not speak again as he went about his work.

REPOSSESSED. Drugged. Sold. Re-sold. Re-drugged. And all that was just the things Kendall had been vaguely awake for. There was probably some steps in-between those. She wasn't sure which was worse—the things she could recall, or the things she couldn't. As she found herself trapped on a ship owned by the Galaxy Brides Corporation for the last month, it seemed her captors had one last stop they wanted her to make on this nightmare of a journey—a Qurilixen marriage ceremony.

Kendall remembered waking up in a medic unit in some bumpy transport, crammed into a tight storage box and in a stasis chamber. She supposed it could have been much worse. Maybe it was much worse. She didn't know how long she'd been unconscious, or how many days had passed by under the exchanging hands of her keepers. It wasn't like people aged in stasis, but to keep a person under for too long risked a horrible death. The last she'd heard the medical alliance was unable to cure stasis sickness.

What if they had done something to her while she slept? With a medic unit to fix her, she wouldn't be able to tell. What if her father lost Margot in the same way? What if her little sister was trapped in a transport box?

Each thought caused her heart to beat faster until the fear choked her and her world spun. How long had she been unconscious? No one would tell her. Maybe they didn't know. Maybe they just didn't care. The second her father had signed her over, she had become property, and everyone she met treated her as such.

She forced a deep breath and then another, trying to calm herself so she could think. The one date she'd managed to discover wasn't one she could understand without access to a conversion chart. On the fueling dock they'd not had much use for measuring time like those who lived on worlds. Sure, her family kept record of days in their own way, but with so many travelers using so many different types of record-keeping, and with computers so readily available should a conversion be necessary—which was never really the case— she had never bothered to memorize intergalactic date-conversion charts. Until now, the idea of actually uploading millions upon millions of tedious charts into her brain had seemed about as worthless as uploading hand-cooking techniques. Not once in her thirty years had she needed to convert time, or cook without aid of a food simulator.

Her situation was unbearable, yet she had no choice but to carry on and do what she was told. It wasn't as if she'd eject herself into deep space with only a life pod and no sense of where she was.

The same thoughts had swirled through her

brain, ever since she'd woken up on the luxury spacecraft. She vaguely remembered hearing of the primitive planet of Qurilixen in her fuel-ore studies. Everything else had been uploaded into her brain by the corporation, and she couldn't help but wonder at the accuracy of those facts—after all, they were a business with the sole purpose of trying to sell brides to grooms. Located in the isolated space of the Y quadrant, the far-flung world was a veritable prison populated by warrior men whose genetics didn't seem to include propagating females. The Draig weren't star voyagers, and for all Kendall knew they wouldn't have access to spaceships.

However, that wasn't the worst part. Not only would she be stranded on the planet with these warrior men, without money, without means, without anything but the clothes on her back, she was expected to marry one of them so the company could recoup her father's debt and make a profit. Turning her head toward the metal corridor wall as she walked passed, she stared at the bold words that read, *Galaxy Brides Corporation— Joining Hearts Across the Universes.*

"Hearts," she repeated softly. "This cargo ship has nothing to do with hearts."

Kendall was a business transaction. Plain and simple. The Draig men of Qurilixen needed women to produce children. They were the buyers. She was the merchandise. Galaxy Brides was the broker. As she saw it, the fate was almost as bad as if they'd sold her into bondage on a pleasure ship. Only, this way, she would be expected to please one man, not many.

"What happens when I can't please him?" she whispered. Growing up on a fueling dock, she had plenty of experience dealing with any number of alien species during the course of her work. The problem was no one had really stayed around long enough to even begin a long-term relationship. Kendall had never been comfortable with the idea of sleeping with a man she didn't know, so the few boyfriends she had had were fueling dock regulars who'd came through on shipping runs. Instead of nurturing those mediocre sexual relationships, she'd buried herself in her work, in her school and in taking care of Margot.

School. There was another thing she wouldn't be able to finish, and she was so close to getting certified by the Exploratory Science Commission as a Fuelologist and Station Engineer. It had taken her nearly six years of virtual-class time to get as far as she had.

Round and round her mind spun—Margot, school, home, marriage to a stranger. She'd been all over the high skies in her lifetime, yet she wasn't that worldly. She had grown up on a fueling dock, traveling, but never staying for too long in one place, and she normally only saw planets from a small window.

A knot formed in her stomach. Life on a planet. She used to dream of it, but now it terrified her. One planet. One place.

"What about Margot? She won't know where I am." The sound of her own voice was oddly comforting, more so than the overly excited voices of her travel companions echoing from the ship's beauty parlor. The rest of the prospective brides were getting ready for the official docking later that evening.

"I'm Aeron, not Margot," a woman answered. The long length of her black hair was pulled away from her reserved face. "I don't think we've met."

"Kendall."

"Are you excited for the ceremony, Kendall?"

Kendall blinked, nodding in agreement as she pulled her arms around her waist and looked at the floor to hide the fact she was lying. It wasn't that she didn't like the woman. Kendall just had nothing to say to any of the women on the ship. When she didn't elaborate on her answer, Aeron hurried past, leading the way to the expansive beauty parlor. Kendall followed behind, watching the other woman's heels.

As far as Kendall could tell, she was the only one forced to be on the ship. The other brides were being well compensated for their participation. They had answered an advertisement and chosen to be here. In fact, they all seemed to think it was some sort of grand vacation. They had spent the last month being pampered and primped for the coming night—the Qurilixen Breeding Festival. Looking down at her toes, she saw the permanent pale-pink color on her nails. It was just one of the many things they'd done to her. She'd had medical scans, health checks, cosmetic dentistry, permanent hair removal, a body-enhancing lift. Running her tongue over her teeth, it felt weird there was no longer a chip in the canine.

"I wish I could be so ambitious. I'm afraid I didn't watch a single one of those boring uploads."

Kendall glanced up at the sound. The women were talking about marriage, as usual. Seeing an empty chair in the shadowed corner away from the others, she sat down. The beauty droid automatically activated and went to work on her hair. Those around her were in various stages of completion.

Whoever spoke referred to the uploads in the ship's computer. If you weren't used to them, they could give a wicked migraine, but Kendall had utilized them for her schooling. They were great for uploading factual information directly into the brain, such as cultural information or a new language. They weren't so good when it came to practical applications. Why hadn't she just paid the extra fee for the conversion-chart uploads?

"Don't look so worried," Trinia said, pausing on her way past. None of the women seemed to know Kendall's name, but she knew theirs. "I've been married over thirty times. There's nothing to it."

Kendall said nothing. Marriage wasn't the only thing Trinia had done over thirty times. The woman's shiny skin looked as if it had been over-enhanced to the point of plasticity.

"I'll tell you a secret," Trinia continued, lowering her voice. She leaned close to Kendall's ear. Kendall stiffened to feel the woman's breath on her skin. She smelled of liquor and spicy meat. "If you don't like them, divorce them and keep the presents. Or don't let them ask you to marry them. If they don't ask, you can't get into trouble for saying no. Then Galaxy Brides will give you a ride to the next planet if you want. If you do it right, you can travel the universe for years until they catch on."

Kendall didn't answer. Trinia laughed, flinging her hand carelessly as she sauntered away.

"This is not my life," Kendall whispered,

desperately wishing she was back on the fueling dock.

Thanks to the uploads her captors had forced on her, Kendall's head was filled with Qurilixian facts. Indeed, she still had a small headache from the rush of information. They were classified as a warrior class, though they had been peaceful for nearly a century—aside from petty territorial skirmishes that broke out every fifteen or so years between a few of the rival houses. The planet was on the outer edge of the Y quadrant, inhabited by primitive males similar to Viking clans of Medieval Earth—not that she knew what those were. The Qurilixian worshipped many gods, favored natural comforts to modern technological conveniences and actually preferred to cook their own food. They called their wedding ceremony a Breeding Festival and it was only allowed to happen at night. The planet only had one night a year and it would begin in a few hours.

The only interesting fact was that their mines were one of the only mineral-rich sources of the *galaxa-promethium* in the known universes. It was a semi-radioactive element that not only had stable isotopes, but whose components could be harnessed to fuel long-voyaging starships. The resulting fuel was so expensive that her family didn't bother to stock it. Normally, only very trivial amounts of the element could be found in nature. Qurilixen was loaded with it.

"I tried on my gown this afternoon," Gena, another bride, said. The woman pushed up her generous chest beneath the robe. "They are gorgeous, but I think I am going to go get my breasts enhanced again—just a little bigger—and I'm going to have my nipples enlarged. Those princes won't be able to resist me. Maybe I'll marry all four of them, just for fun."

"How will you know who the princes are?" a blonde asked from across the room. The women were obsessed by the fact royalty was going to be at the ceremony looking for wives. "I've heard that all the men wear disguises. You could end up with a royal guard."

"Or a gardener," offered a brunette with a laugh.

"I hear they wear practically nothing at all," added a woman with flaming red hair and sparkling green eyes the color of emeralds. "Except the mask and some fur."

"You can't miss royalty," Gena said with a kittenish smile of excitement. It was hard to miss Gena. She made sure everyone knew her name. "You'll see it in the way they move."

Kendall looked down at her own robe and pulled it tighter across her chest, trying to hide her new body. Since she was bought and paid for, the company had automatically put her through certain procedures. The new breasts were real, just genetically altered for perfection.

Her beauty droid pulled her hair and she was forced to look back up. Their spacecraft was outfitted with the best accommodations and services the star system had to offer. Personal droids were assigned to each passenger, and cooking units in each of their quarters could materialize almost any culinary delight without straying from the strict mineral diets the corporation had them on. Even the doctor was mechanical.

As the droids finished, the prospective brides began to slowly make their way back to their personal quarters to dress. Kendall had been assigned a later appointment in the ship's logs and would be one of the last to finish her treatments. Closing her eyes, she waited as many of the women left the beauty parlor. She let loose a nervous breath and wished it would all just go away.

2

Run.

The command made absolutely no logical sense and yet Kendall could do nothing else. Her instincts said run and her feet obeyed. The dark red soil passed under her as she made her way from the Galaxy Brides' ship. The tight black of her clothing clung to her new body like a second skin, helping her to blend in to the darkened surroundings. Dusk swept along the reddish-brown earth, shadowing oversized leaves on thick branches. The foliage began to droop, as if resting after a long year of light, as darkness finally came to Qurilixen.

Run faster.

Kendall ran faster. Somehow she'd managed to sneak off the ship while the other brides were getting dressed for the ceremony. Dumb luck.

That's what it had been. Dumb luck that the beauty droid needed a repair and had reported to maintenance, leaving Kendall unattended. Dumb luck that the docking plank had been opened for the ship's staff before the brides were ready to descend into the campground. Dumb luck that the locals weren't around to catch her as she sneaked down the plank. And perhaps simply dumb that she now ran through an alien forest to escape the fate of marriage.

Faster.

Her heart pounded. She wasn't a runner. There weren't open fields on a fueling dock. It didn't stop her from moving. It would appear the Galaxy Brides' treatments had expanded her lung capacity and strengthened her muscles. The forest became darker. What was she doing? Soon she wouldn't be able to see.

Kendall slowed to a jog before stopping in front of a fallen log. The thick trunk was too big to jump over. Pressing her hand against the bark, she gasped for breath. Tears entered her eyes. She needed to find a way off world. She needed to get to Margot before her father gambled the child away, before her father fell so deep into a hole he couldn't claw his way out. Flawed or not, the man was family.

The only comfort was that legally her father

would have to be in debt for several months before the casino could issue another repossession order. But then she had no way of knowing how much time had passed while she'd been in stasis. Surely they hadn't kept her in storage that long. They wouldn't have wanted to risk stasis sickness by keeping her under sedation. Margot should be safe.

What if she wasn't? Kendall couldn't begin to translate any of the alien timekeeping methods. What if Margot had already been sold into captivity? Her sister was too young to be a bride. The thought brought little comfort. There were much worse things than marriage.

Just run.

ALEK LED the procession of bridegrooms over the familiar path to make his offering to the gods. It was not lost on him how useless the task felt this year. It was as if all hope had finally withered. Even last year, there had been a small thread of excitement. Now, nothing. He'd gone dead inside. He just wanted it to be over.

Perhaps it was for the best. He would go through the motions, make his offering, stand in line and then sneak off to the pre-arranged campsite to meet up with his brothers to drink away his heartache. Well, all but one of his brothers. Vladan had found a woman right before the ceremony was to start. The fact did not give Alek hope. Though his brother in every way that mattered, Vladan had been born of different parents and adopted by Alek's father after his parents had been killed in a mining accident when he was very young.

Before the ceremony, the king had ordered the men be presented to the marriageable daughter of a friend of one of the mining dignitaries. Apparently, Lady Clara of the Redding was above attending their *primitive* festival and refused to marry beneath her station. She'd barely even acknowledged them as she coldly looked over the highest ranking nobles the Draig had to offer. In fact, when Vladan's crystal had begun to glow, she'd merely tilted her head, turned her back on them and left the main area of the tent. Perhaps Vladan was not so blessed. Which was worse—a cold bride or no bride?

"At least a cold bride can thaw with time and warmth," he whispered, balling his hands into fists.

Alek looked at his hands, but the familiar lines of his callused palms held no answers. Perhaps his blood was tainted. Only the gods could know their reasons. The gods did not feel the need to tell their reasons to a mortal like him.

Stopping before the temple, he couldn't bring

himself to step inside. The others passed by him, going in. They focused on their own ceremonies and didn't pay attention to him. Only his brother Mirek stopped and questioned, "Alek?"

"I need relief," he answered, turning to the forest. Mirek chuckled but did not stop him.

The fur loincloth gave little protection as he moved into the forest. Thick brush rubbed against his thighs, scratching his skin. Alek didn't care. He couldn't make himself go into the temple to beg the gods for something that was not to be. He couldn't. Not again. He accepted his loveless fate and saw no reason to continue to fight it. Surely the gods could respect such a decision. He acknowledged their ruling that he was destined to be alone. If that was what fate had in store for him, so be it. He would not torture himself further.

His eyes shifted to gold and his vision cut through the darkness as if it were daylight. The dragon form inside of him made it easier to sense the forest. As the skin of his thighs hardened with protective armor, the brush no longer irritated his flesh and he was able to move faster.

He reached for his neck, jerking the crystal that hung there. The leather strap broke. Fingering the stone, he traced over the familiar surface before balling it into his fist. He thought about leaving it on the forest floor, as if his failure would be easier to bear without the constant reminder hanging about his neck. As he debated the decision his fist became warm, then hot. Loosening his grip, he saw the faint glow of light radiating from between his fingers.

The crystal glowed.

Alek couldn't believe what he was seeing so he merely stared at it. He was in the forest. Alone.

Alone?

He held his breath and let the hard, dark-brown flesh of the dragon work its way from his thighs up his body. A ridge grew from his forehead to create a protective shield over his nose and brow. Fangs extended in his mouth and talons grew from his nail beds. In his dragon form, he moved with greater agility and his senses were enhanced.

Was he alone? Was this the final word of the gods?

The crystal's light grew. The sign was unmistakable. His bride had to be near. Even as he thought it, he began to feel her inside him. The pull of her drew him before he picked up the sound of her breathing in the forest. Footfalls hit in a steady rhythm for several paces only to grow softer and slower. The beast inside him surged into action. He tracked her as easily as prey.

He found her standing alone in the dark, body pressed tight against a fallen log. Her widened brown eyes darted around the forest in fear. He stopped across the clearing from her. She didn't see him even though she looked in his direction several times. Alek took advantage of the moment to study her. Blonde hair fell about her shoulders. The ends were tipped with a dark red. She seemed so fragile and scared. A wave of protectiveness surged within him.

"Hayo? I can hear you breathing," she whispered. "Please show yourself. I can hear you."

Alek lifted his hand and opened his fist. The soft glow of the crystal alighted on his face. The woman found him instantly. He expected her to feel the same rush of pleasure he did. Instead, she started to scream.

The woman tripped on vines as she tried to get away from him. Her back slid along the tree trunk. He smelled the moss she disturbed in her haste. She kept her eyes on his and her arms outstretched as if that would keep him from attacking. Her feet worked frantically against the ground, pushing her back up the tree while trying to untangle her shoes from the forest floor.

"Please, no, no, no," she whimpered. "I don't belong here. Who are you people? You're supposed to be humanoids. The uploads said you were shaped like humans."

Alek tried to answer her, but the sound of his

native tongue only seemed to terrify her more. He realized he was still shifted. No wonder she was frightened. He'd been so eager to find her that he hadn't bothered to change back. His people did not make their shifting abilities too widely known, and they hadn't revealed them to the researcher who'd originally interviewed his people for the uploads she spoke of.

"I don't understand." She pressed harder into the wood. "They didn't have us upload any native-language data. I only speak the star language."

With little effort, he allowed his body to mold into a form she would be more comfortable with. Flesh replaced the hard shell of his skin. His fangs retracted, as did his talons. When he'd finished the transformation only his golden eyes remained so that he could see her in the darkened forest.

"I am Lord Aleksej, Younger Duke of Draig," he said in the universal star language, trying to keep the eagerness from his voice. Like shifting and other secrets of his planet, the Draig did not share their language—not that anyone other than the locals wanted to learn it. "How did you come to be in the forest?"

"What are you, Lord Aleksej, Younger Duke of Draig?" she whispered, still pressing tight into the fallen tree.

"You may call me Alek. I am Draig, a dragon-shifter. Do not let my appearance before frighten you. I mean you no harm." He took a careful step closer, lifting the crystal toward her. "I was meant to find you."

"Galaxy Brides sent you to track me," she said, as if knowing this to be a truth. "You can tell them you didn't find me. You can tell them I disappeared. I won't hurt anyone. I just want to go home. Please, you can understand that, can't you? I don't want to go to the ceremony. I just want to find a ride home. Please don't make me go back."

The woman wasn't dressed as a bride, but neither was he dressed fully like a groom. He didn't wear the mask. They shouldn't be talking, not like this. There were traditions. Though tradition allowed him to find a mate whenever the crystal glowed, he wasn't supposed to speak to her on the festival night until she made the symbolic gesture of choosing him.

"Please," she begged.

"Come with me," he answered. "I'll take you to my tent. You can wait there during the procession. You will be safe."

Alek wasn't about to let her walk through the line. What if the gods decided to give her to someone else? No. This woman was his. He wasn't going to risk losing her. Besides, she looked terrified.

"I promise on my family's honor, you will be safe there."

"Thank you," she answered after some hesitation. She didn't readily move.

"Come," he said, already worried he'd said too much. "I promise you will be safe."

She walked silently behind him as he led her toward the valley of tents set up in the festival grounds. He wanted to touch her, to kiss her, to hold her. He refrained. He had found her. That was enough for now. Already his passions stirred within him, growing beneath the loincloth. Soon he would possess all of her.

Finally. The gods had blessed him.

WHAT IN ALL of the known universes was she doing?

Kendall didn't think following the shifter man was the best idea. Unfortunately, she had little choice but to trust him. The forest had darkened fast, making it so she couldn't see. When she'd heard him approach she'd been convinced that some beast had come to kill her. She had never been so terrified in her life. Planet life was so open, so vast, not like the confined comfort of the spaceship. On a fueling dock the population could be controlled. Everyone who landed and took off were logged and tracked. If she was worried, she had the authority to look up a visitor's record. Here, on a planet, creatures could roam at will, unlogged, unhampered. Even though she had spent many hours as a bored young girl daydreaming of an existence on world, in reality she was not built for planet life.

The glowing stone he held outlined him with soft light. She kept her eyes on Alek's back. It was hard to see, but he walked slowly and she was able to stumble along with minimal effort.

Slowly, lights began to poke through the thick foliage. As they neared the campgrounds, she began to relax. Giant blazing fires combined with moonlight to make the area light enough to see. The smell of burning wood mingled with the scent of earth and trees. She paused when she saw the Galaxy Brides' ship, but her companion walked in the opposite direction.

"Come," he said, not turning to look at her. She wondered how he knew she'd stopped walking. She wasn't being loud.

Torches lit dim earthen pathways leading through the large triangular tents beyond the main clearing. Ribbons and banners floated on the breeze in many brilliant colors. The tents were illuminated from within and the flickering firelight through canvas caressed the surrounding area with a diffused light. Alek stopped before one of the tents, lifted the flap and waited. Kendall glanced around the campsite before ducking inside.

"You will be safe here. Wait and I will come back for you after the bridal procession." With that, he closed the flap and left her. He didn't wait for her to agree.

The ground inside was covered with fur. Torchlight sputtered around her. The smaller space gave her some comfort when compared to the greatness of the outdoors. At least, it did until she looked around. A giant bed was in the middle of the room. She'd never seen a bed so big. Onboard the fueling dock her bed was only big enough to fit one person. The Draig bed could easily hold her five times over. Gauze hung around it, cocooning it in hazy softness.

A tub of hot water waited in one corner. She knew it was for bathing, though she'd never tried a water bath. In space, laser baths were a much more efficient use of ship resources. The next corner held pleasure toys—oils, whips, straps, soft plush ties and various other objects. She recognized them from traveling sale ships that came through with their wares, trying to sell their goods off of holographic demonstrations and advertisements. The last corner had food. She went to that one and studied the piles of chocolate and pitchers of wine. Chocolate? She moved her finger to touch one. Chocolate was so rare in space. She'd only had it once as a child. Monks had come trying to convert them and handed the temptations out like they were the keys to paradise. It was so delicious she'd remembered the taste even now, years later. She wondered why the people who programmed the food simulators didn't include the treat in their menus. Kendall glanced around the primitive tent. These men must be rich indeed to have plates of chocolate just lying around unguarded. The monks had told her that wars broke out over the stuff, for it was the food of the gods.

Of course she wanted to try one, but she forced her hand back. She couldn't steal from him, not when she hoped Alek would help her find a way home.

Kendall closed her eyes. Alek was not a man she wanted to anger. She'd seen him shifted. It was a sight she wouldn't soon forget. Though, seeing him as a man, she wasn't sure which state was more frightening. He'd been very comfortable in his half-naked state, and she had been decidedly uncomfortable with it. Bare feet, strong legs, defined back and chest, thick arms… The image did something euphorically wicked to her on a primal level, something she could never act upon.

Opening her eyes, she took a deep, steadying breath. Perhaps a small drink of wine would be all right. One sip to steady her nerves.

IT TOOK every bit of self-restraint Alek had to keep a calm expression as the brides began to filter through the receiving line. The potential husbands were lined up in two rows, creating a path the women were to walk through. This was the moment he was supposed to find his bride amongst those from the ship.

Alek held his hand around his crystal, covering its glow so no one would see it before it was time. He didn't want his brothers asking questions. He didn't want anyone to know he had hid his new bride away in a tent for fear the gods would take her from him. Such a reaction to fear was not an honorable act. He should have brought her back to the line, let her walk through with the other women as was tradition. Never in his life had he panicked as he had tonight. The others would have understood their chance meeting. Finding a bride before the ceremony occasionally happened, but they still followed tradition.

However, Alek had waited too long to find his

fate. He could not let her go now. He could not risk it. The fear was unreasonable, but it was there.

Like the other grooms, he wore the mask over his face from forehead to upper lip and a gold band around his biceps. As over half the alien brides passed by him, he released the glowing crystal. It blended with the other lucky grooms whose mates had been chosen by fate. His brother Bron had been blessed, as had the four princes. However, Mirek had not. Vladan was not in line, having received a royal pardon due to his bride's unique situation.

When all of the prospective brides had passed, Alek went to where his two brothers stood.

"I will attend to the campsite before traveling home," Mirek was saying to Bron as Alek approached. "I will not wait for you. Enjoy your good fortune."

Mirek's attention turned to the glowing crystal at Alek's chest. He nodded and tried to smile, but his eyes were filled with a deep sadness. "Many blessings on your union, brother."

Alek started to speak, but there was nothing he could say to ease Mirek's suffering. He knew that all too well. Mirek walked away, heading toward the high cliff where they normally made camp after a failed attempt. Tonight, Mirek would sleep there alone.

"Is all well?" Bron asked him when they were alone enough to speak.

Alek gave a small laugh, but the effort was forced. Worry filled him as he thought of the woman hidden in his tent. What if someone found her? What if she left? "What could be wrong? Three of us have been blessed, as well as all of our princely cousins. For whatever reason, the gods have finally decided to smile upon us. It is a good night for all but Mirek. Let us give thanks and collect our brides before the gods realize what they have done and change their minds."

"Don't even think such things," Bron scolded. His brother gave him a stern look and then turned to follow the other blessed grooms as they made their way back to the temple.

Alek started to follow, but halfway there found himself turning toward the tents. He slipped through the paths, doing his best not to pass by any of the servants milling about the area. His skin hardened in warning. He focused his attention, letting his hearing zone in on his tent, instinctively knowing something was not right.

"You are coming with us, Girl One Haven," a male voice ordered from within Alek's tent. "You have a debt to repay."

"It's not my debt," his bride answered. "How many times do I have to say it?"

"Then you should have filed a grievance with the repossession company," the man answered. "There are proper channels to be followed. We have confirmation of your legal sale."

Alek sprinted into action, running the distance to his tent, not caring who saw him.

"Grievance? When?" his bride demanded. "I was unconscious the whole time!"

"You are the property of Galaxy Brides until such a time as you are chosen," another man answered. "We're taking you to the unmarried grooms. You know the deal, Kendall Haven. Find one here or we have orders to transport you on to the next destination."

Two men tried to pull Alek's bride through the front flap. Kendall kicked violently, landing a few blows. But she did not manage to free herself as they forced her to go with them.

"Unhand my bride," Alek ordered, enraged. He jerked the mask from his face to better see the two men should they choose to fight. One was slight of build and looked better suited to a dignitary position, but the other stood nearly as tall as a Draig and had the physique of a soldier.

The men stopped, stunned to silence. Kendall swung, hitting the smaller man square in the jaw. The other released her and stepped to the side. The men shared a look.

The larger man said, "Our apologies. Her tracker indicated she was not at the ceremony. We did not know she had been chosen. We'll report her marital status to our superiors."

The other man rubbed his jaw. He gave Kendall a sour look as he reached into a hidden pocket on his red uniform. Pulling out a small device, he gestured it toward Alek before setting it on the ground. "This device will track her. We'll mark the transaction as completed. She is yours now and we are no longer liable for her care or keep. If she gives you trouble, report it. For a fee we can track her in space and bring her back."

"Just leave," Kendall said under her breath. Her eyes turned to the ground, but her body was tense with anger. She looked ready to pounce.

The men gave Alek a wide berth as they hurried toward the docked luxury ship. Kendall breathed hard, not looking up until they were gone. She held up her hand. The knuckles were red and she flexed her fingers. Meeting Alek's eyes, she said, "Thank you. I didn't realize they had put a tracker inside me, but I guess I should have known."

"We can't talk out here," he said, picking up the tracker the men had left before ushering her inside the privacy of the tent.

"The device is embedded into my hand." She kept talking as he closed them inside. Her eyes stayed on the tracking unit as he tossed it on the bed. "I felt heat radiating in my palm when they came for me. I am sorry to have involved you, but I am grateful for your help in sending them away." She nervously looked from the tracker to her hand. "I don't know how I'm going to get the tracking chip out. Or even the range of the thing." She began pressing her finger into her palm, feeling around. "I guess…a knife?"

Alek crossed to her and grabbed her hand. "You are not cutting your hand."

Kendall blinked in surprise. "I won't do it in here if that's what you're worried about, but I can't leave the tracker in. I won't bleed on your belongings and I will bring the knife back."

"You are my wife. I will make arrangements to have the tracker disabled safely by those who are trained to do so." He pressed his mask into her hand. "Take this. It belongs to you." Then he picked up the tracking unit and also gave it to her. "And this as well."

"Wife?" She looked at the mask and unit in her hands, then his face. "I think there has been a misunderstanding. I am not marrying you, Alek. I can't. I have to get off this planet. I can't stay here. It's too…"

"What?" he questioned a little too harshly.

"On world," she finished weakly. The statement

was more of a question. She was nervous, maybe even scared.

His nerves tingled and his muscles threatened to shift into dragon form. Heightened emotions surged within him. The warrior wanted to go after the men and fight. The groom forced himself to relax. This was a blessed night, no time for fighting. He softened his tone, refocusing his attention where it belonged. "You are missing the bridal feast. Shall I order food brought for you?"

"I'm not hungry," she said, even as she glanced at the food table. "Honestly, I just want to go home. I'm so tired. I've been awake for days."

He considered her for a long moment. Finally, he nodded. "There is nowhere to go tonight." He touched her cheek. "Lie on the bed. Rest. I will take you home tomorrow."

Kendall looked at his crystal and then back up to meet his gaze. Slowly, she pulled her face from his hand. He hadn't noticed the tired marks under her eyes or the sleep-deprived red edging the brown irises. Normally he was observant, but he'd been so excited to have finally found her he had missed her need for rest.

"I won't be able to sleep, even if I do need it. Every time I try, I..." She didn't meet his gaze and he wondered at it. "Thank you, but I have imposed too long already."

"Rest," he repeated. "No one will harm you here. The festival ground is no place for a tired bride. They will be drinking well into the night in celebration. If it is rest you seek, this is the best place for you."

She swayed lightly on her feet. "All right. You saved me twice—from the forest and from those men. I have no reason not to trust your word. I can sleep on the floor. I don't wish to put you out of your bed."

Relief filled him now that she no longer spoke of getting off his planet.

"The floor is no place for you," he said. "Take the bed. Rest."

Kendall considered the unit in her hand. She went to a chair along the edge of the tent and tilted it back so a leg came off the ground. She placed the unit underneath the leg and slammed it down. The casing dented so she could pry it off and expose the delicate insides of the device. This time when she crushed it with the chair leg it gave a loud electrical pop and then died.

He laughed. "I would say it is disabled."

"I have no use for it, but I clearly have cause to disable it." Kendall set the broken pieces on the floor near the edge of the tent, out of the way. "Are you sure you don't mind me taking the bed?"

"I insist upon it."

She considered him for a moment before moving toward the bed. She kicked off her shoes and pulled back the fur coverlet to crawl onto the high mattress. Stretching out on her side, she studied him. "No one will come in?"

"I will make sure of it," he told her, though he knew no one would come unless summoned. She sighed at his reassurance, and he hid his small smile of pleasure to know she trusted his word without question. It was a very good sign as to their future together.

"Thank you, Alek." She rolled over, putting her back toward him.

Alek took the three torches from the walls and dipped them into the bath water, putting out the fires. The tent became dark and quiet. There was soft glow from the outside bonfires shining through the wall. It bathed the slope of her form in the gentlest of orange lights. In the years to come, he was sure he would always remember the way she looked in this moment.

My bride.

Alek helped himself to wine while he listened to her breathing. He knew the moment she started to slip into a deep sleep. Setting the goblet down, the wine in it unfinished, he lightly touched the glowing crystal. This was not how he'd imagined his marriage ceremony. Most men believed there would be moments of discovery, touching and kissing, whispering and playing, and a bit of pleasurable-torture as their new brides did their own exploring. Still, he would not complain. If sleep was what his bride desired, then sleep was what she would have. With the blood pumping in his veins, granting her request was not as easy as it first appeared. He wanted to touch her and feel her and taste her.

The bed was large enough to hold them both and he crawled next to her and lay on top of the fur coverlet. He made no move to hold her. For now he would be content that she was in his tent, that his crystal glowed and that finally the gods had seen fit to send him a wife.

3

KENDALL KNEW she was not safe in her quarters the moment her mind woke from her dreams. Her bed did not feel like this one. Her room was not so warm. In those first gradual seconds, she expected to be jarred by her captors into the harsh reality of her new life. Where were they keeping her now? Did it even matter?

She opened her eyes to her dark surroundings and felt momentary confusion at the peacefulness of them. No tight space or metal walls closed her in. No stasis chamber. No ship's prison hold. The soft orange glow along the wall was the only light. It flickered, coming from a fire outside of the canvas enclosure. Kendall was amazed she'd slept. Normally the fear of being helplessly stuck back into stasis kept her mind alert. Her eyes adjusted and she was able to discern the surrounding shadows—a table, the platter of chocolate, a pitcher. She slid her hand to her mouth. A strange material was clutched in her fingers. As it neared her nose she detected a familiar smell. Alek. His mask. The material tangled in her fingers.

Kendall pushed up on the bed and tried to make out shapes on the floor. Then, looking behind her, she found what she was searching for. Alek was on the bed next to her. He rested on top of the coverlet. Since she was beneath it, the material kept them from touching. She detected the outline of his form. Muscles formed ridges in the flesh. His arm lifted above his head, framing his face and drawing her attention to his parted lips and strong nose. She stared, mesmerized by the look of him.

Perhaps it was the sleepy haze she was under, or the quiet surrealism of the tent, or even the relief of no longer being under the thumb of her captors. She reached to him and let her finger move down the slope of his nose. Kendall shivered, as if that touch proved this was real and she was finally free. It was a light touch but she could feel his heat against her cooler skin. She traced the divot above his lip then along the seam of his mouth to his chin. His eyes blinked open and he looked first at the ceiling before slowly turning his gaze toward her. The shadows hid his eyes when he looked at her until a hint of gold pierced the darkness. He'd shifted his eyes into that of the dragon.

"Thank you for saving me from them," she whispered. She moved her hand to his neck. The intimate moment seemed natural somehow. The crystal glowed brighter, casting his shadowed features into light.

"What did they want with you? Why were they tracking you?" he asked.

She liked the sound of his voice. It was low, almost gruff, yet soothing. She couldn't bring herself to answer. Her eyes searched for the tracking unit, finding it broken on the floor where she'd left it. The truth was too humiliating. How could she say her father had signed her over to a casino to cover a gambling debt? She knew her father loved her, in his way, but he'd lost her in a game of chance. *A game.* "They made a mistake, but no amount of protesting seemed to make a difference. I'm sure you know how those types of companies operate. They are too large and the departments don't talk to each other. My protests were ignored. They thought they had the right to bring me here as a bride. It doesn't matter. They've left thanks to you. It's finally over. I don't think I can ever repay you for your kindness."

He rolled onto his side. The move forced her fingers to fall across his collarbone onto the bed. A hand came for her and he touched her as she had him. Lightly, he traced her nose and mouth, dipping over the curve of her chin to her throat. His finger paused by her pulse, as if gauging the pace of her heart as it beat a rhythm in her neck. "You are safe with me."

"You have already done so much, I hate to ask for one more thing." She was well aware of his touch. Her heart quickened and she felt herself leaning closer to him. "Can you help me find a ship willing to give me passage to the X Quadrant? It's important."

"What is in the X?"

"My home. I don't have anyone else I can ask." She covered his hand with hers, holding him against her neck. "I give you my word that I will pay you for your trouble once I get back. I don't have much, but I am good to my word."

"I cannot send you to the X. I'm sorry." He moved his finger along her jaw line.

"I understand." Kendall tried not to let her disappointment show. She would just have to find another means of travel. It was quite possible this man didn't have the funds to lend her the passage fare to another quadrant. It would be an expensive trip. This wedding ceremony probably cost the participating men a great deal. The plate of chocolate alone could easily equal the price of a flight off world. Knowing Alek would not have a bride to show for it, she felt sorry for him.

"I have a good home," he offered.

Kendall covered his mouth before he could say more. She knew what he would offer. This was a bridal ceremony after all. His whole purpose in participating would be to find a wife. Really it was sad. These poor men had to settle for whoever would have them because fate had taken away their female children. What a horrible way to find a partner. She could just imagine some of the nutcases who agreed to this. Actually, she didn't need to imagine. She had seen them on the ship. Riona, the degenerate gambler always making wagers on the most mundane things. Olena, who acted more like a pirate than a bride. Gina, with her enormous breasts and nauseatingly horrific laugh. Trinia, a woman constructed of biological plastic.

"What are you thinking?" He touched the center of her forehead where her brows had furrowed together in concentration.

"Of how I'm going to find a way home," she said.

"Everything will work out the way it is meant to," he assured her. Alek leaned toward her. His lips neared hers until she could feel the gentle brush of his breath against her mouth. She didn't move, mesmerized by the glow reflecting in his eyes. He kissed her lightly, sweeping his mouth gently across hers.

This was new territory for her. She didn't move, only stared at him, waiting to see what he intended to do next. He kissed her again, moving his lips firmly against hers. Arousal and awareness unfurled inside her. Alek captivated her senses, holding them hostage as she awaited his next move. The third kiss lingered as he parted his lips. The action urged her to mimic his movements. She sucked in a shaky breath. Alek ran his tongue along the seam of her mouth. The feeling was wickedly decadent.

Kendall wasn't some sheltered recluse. She knew what he wanted from her. Her body wanted it too. Luckily for her body, her mind didn't seem to be working at the moment.

Alek kissed her again and probed his tongue deeper still. He let his hand travel down her throat to her chest. The material of her shirt did little to protect her from his heat. He cupped a breast, running a thumb over the already sensitive nipple. He moved his fingers slowly over her chest, along her collarbone to tease her aware flesh. Her eyes closed. She inhaled a deep breath, silently willing his hand more fully against her breast.

He traced the tip of his tongue along the seam of her mouth to entice her to participate in his plans. Kendall inched closer. She wanted to feel more of him.

Alek's touch stayed light and teasing. He explored the curve of her side and hip before reaching around to cup her ass. She gasped into his mouth as the hard, unmistakable press of his arousal fitted against her. The intimacy of the act took her by surprise. She'd never been held so intensely, as if each of his breaths depended on hers.

The feel of male flesh was intoxicating. Since he only wore the fur loincloth, there was nothing to stop her hands from journeying over tight peaks and valleys. Muscles flexed as he moved subtly against her. He slid his knee between her thighs. She clamped her legs, automatically trying to stop him. It was useless. A thick thigh pressed up into her sex and she gasped at the way he rubbed against her.

A low moan sounded as he deepened the kiss. Their tongues began to war, fighting for control. Hands pulled and grabbed. She heard the rip of cloth seconds before feeling strong fingers on her naked body. Torn material tickled where it still clung to her. Alek massaged her butt and drew her forward so that her softer skin molded around the erect length of his shaft. The fur loincloth padded them, keeping them apart.

Alek groaned, pausing long enough to jerk the impeding material aside. With the cushion of fur gone, she now felt his length in long, intimate detail. He breathed heavily, "*ah, woman,*" before rocking harder. Almost mindlessly, he tugged at her waist to force her pants down her ass and hip. With his leg between her thighs, he couldn't undress her further. His cock hit her exposed hip and stomach.

The pressure of his leg along her slit and the sound of his harsh breathing stoked the fire inside her. Self-pleasure had never felt like this. She made a weak noise and grabbed hold of his arm as his hand kept her tightly to him.

"We must…" He moaned before rocking faster. The hand on her ass moved to her hair and he roughly pulled her head back. Her chest arched and he instantly lowered his mouth to suck a peaked nipple between his lips.

Kendall tensed. It was too much. The pull of her hair, the tug of his mouth, the press of his thigh, they flooded her with pleasure.

"We must not finish." The words were a growl against her breast. "We are only meant to discover each other, learn, reveal ourselves completely, but we are not supposed to finish."

She was barely listening. Kendall hooked her leg around the back of his knee. The angle of her body opened her to the most gratifying of sensations. "Oh, please, please, please," she begged as her body was pushed over the edge of pleasure.

"By all the gods!" Alek swore.

She trembled against him, every muscle tense and every jerk of her body uncontrollable. Sticky warmth flooded her stomach as he found release. When she touched him, her fingers glided over his sweat-beaded flesh. Her hand found his ass. He groaned, jerking again as another wave of wet heat erupted between them.

Alek gasped for breath and whispered, "By all the gods, Kendall. We should not have done that."

He hardly sounded disappointed. In fact, the way he held her tight said he quite enjoyed what they had done. Her heart pounded wildly.

"There is nothing about this night that is going as it should," he continued.

Her eyes moved down to his crystal. She breathed hard. Without giving it much thought, she said, "Is the phosphorescence caused by the night time? I know some phosphorus fuels have such properties, though they are rare."

"You wish to know about the crystal? Now?" Alek gave a small laugh. He reached between them, not bothering to pull their bodies apart. Lifting the crystal, he traced her lips with it. The cool stone contrasted the heat coming off their bodies. She felt the slight buzz of electrical current in the stone.

"I was given this crystal when I was born. My father dove to the bottom of Crystal Lake, plucked it from the rock, and it has been with me ever since. And, until you were near me, it has never so much as twinkled."

"How can that be?" She reached to take it from him and stared into its glowing center. She found herself being pulled into its depths.

"The will of the gods," he stated simply. "When our crystal glows we know what fate has chosen for us. It is why we have these ceremonies. The crystal chooses a match, the woman agrees to it and it is done. We trust in the power of the crystal to guide us."

"That doesn't make much sense, scientifically speaking, I mean."

He took the crystal back. A fire ignited in her where he drew slow, lazy circles against her shoulder and throat with the stone. She took a deep breath and closed her eyes.

"The stone reacts to what is naturally between us, showing us the will of our hearts before we are even aware of it ourselves," he whispered. "Or perhaps it is magic, a spell cast by your beauty that I am unable to resist. I have even broken our law by allowing us to finish what we started this night." He glanced down to where the stickiness of their joining was drying between them. "It has to be a spell to make me forget tradition."

"I don't think we did finish." Her eyes move back up to meet his. An ache had settled inside her. "Not really. I mean, I assume by the look of you that you are made to fit against me differently." Why was she suddenly hesitant and blushing like some innocent? Fit against me differently? Had she really just said that like she didn't already know? What was wrong with her? She was normally quite articulate when it came to discussing, well, anything. Unable to think clearly and a little embarrassed by her sudden idiocy, she tried to correct her vague terminology by adding, "Inside me differently."

Never mind, she was suddenly brainless. She knew how sex was supposed to work. So, okay, yeah, she wasn't as experienced as a Galaxy Playmate, but she wasn't a virgin. Why in the high skies was she suddenly speaking like she'd grown up in a laboratory cage?

His eyes narrowed. If she wasn't mistaken, he looked concerned. "You did not meet with pleasure?"

"I'm saying we didn't actually *finish* finish, so surely there is no law broken. We didn't complete the act."

Kendall was pretty sure she should stop talking.

It didn't help that the man next to her was hard to read. Yes, he smiled and frowned, but the gestures were slight and there always seemed to be more behind his eyes.

Alek seemed to contemplate her words for a long moment. A slow smile curved his lips. "I have never considered the custom in such a way. It was always assumed…" He pushed up from the bed, a grin spreading across his features. Jerking the loincloth from underneath his hip, he tossed it off the bed. Already his shaft had begun to enlarge. Before she could react, he had his hands on her pants and was pulling them off her legs.

Kendall made a weak noise. Well, perhaps she had been mistaken. Alek's intent wasn't hard to read at all.

IN THE BACK of his mind, Alek knew the interpretation of what could and could not be done on the wedding night was not as vague as his new bride suggested. Yet, as a man with needs building inside him like an eruption about to surge forth from a thermal pocket in the mines, he couldn't bring himself to argue her logic. To his thinking, the damage, if any, was already done. There was no reason to deny them both. Tomorrow he would atone.

He tossed her pants onto the floor and took her by the hand. If he wasn't mistaken, he saw a slight tinting to her cheeks. Embarrassment? He looked over her body, to the torn shirt hanging about her shoulders. The ripped sides did nothing to hide her perfect breasts from view. Her skin looked soft, exotic, tan and supple. He remembered the feel of her beneath his hands. The texture of her flesh contrasted the hardness of his. She had no reason for embarrassment.

He led her toward the bath, eager to continue their exploration. Pausing near the tub, he pushed the shirt from her shoulders. The crystal pulsed, lightening her face briefly. It was as if the stone sensed the need growing inside of them. She breathed deeply and closed her eyes.

Alek stepped into the water and sank down into the warm depths. He didn't let go of her hand as he waited for her to join him. She gave a nervous glance around the tent before stepping inside the tub. Alek let go, but only so he could lather soap between his hands. As she began to kneel in the water, he stopped her by running his soapy fingers up her thighs. Kendall's breath caught and she remained upright.

Alek took his time, washing her legs, her stomach, her waist and ass. Her hips rotated ever so slightly in the air. Soft sighs escaped her. Next, he found her breasts. Kneeling before her, he ignored the blatant throbbing in his overly tight erection. The water lapped against his sensitive shaft and balls. He lifted her breasts, watching from below as nipples slipped between fingers. The erotic sight nearly did him in. A small shudder of appreciation rolled through him.

"Alek," she whispered. The very sound of his name said in such a way nearly drove him to the brink. She bent her knees and slithered down into his arms. He couldn't resist pressing his face against her stomach. He moved his head into the valley of her breasts. The sting of soap met his tongue.

She pushed into him, forcing him to sit back on his legs. Alek hugged her closer, moving her against his erection. By all that was sacred. The slick feel of her enraptured him until all he could see was her. Surely this was what it meant to be blessed by the gods. Nothing in his life had felt so perfect.

He wanted to thrust inside her but clung to the very last of his common sense to hold back. He would not dishonor her by consummating their relationship completely. Instead, he held her hips and pressed her firmly against his stomach. The length of his arousal kissed her sex. They rocked in perfect unison. Soap and water, hands and flesh, mouths and tongues.

"Mm, Alek," Kendall whispered against his mouth. She held him by the sides of his face, keeping him against her kiss. Their tongues moved alongside each other, dipping and retracting in long, hot strokes.

He held her along her back, his palms flat against her as she rocked into him. Her hands slipped and he lowered his face onto her chest, feeling the wet glide of her breasts against his cheeks. A nipple slipped across his mouth and he quickly pulled it between his teeth. She gasped as he bit lightly.

Alek growled. It would be so easy to finish it, to join with her. The promise of more to come kept him from staking complete claim. She was his. He would have her again. They had a whole lifetime to join physically.

Possession filled him. The crystal's glow illuminated her face. The wet stroke of their bodies shoved them roughly over the edge. They jerked in unison, riding their shared climax to its explosive end. Her hands gripped his shoulders and her heavy, satisfied gasps echoed around him.

"You are a fine wife," he said, grinning.

She pulled back to look at him. Her eyes

searched his. Breathless, she whispered, "What? I told you I don't speak your native language."

"You are beautiful," he answered, slipping back into the star language, having forgotten what he'd said moments before. "I am a lucky man."

4

KENDALL LOOKED out of the tent at the campground. Behind her, Alek slept on the bed. His limbs were spread out, taking up most of the space. For some reason, she couldn't help thinking he must be a man used to sleeping alone, otherwise he would have naturally left her half the bed. A servant walked by carrying folded clothes in his arms. He glanced in her direction but said nothing as he went to another tent to drop off his bundle. Kendall had found a dress, matching tunic shirt and male pants outside the tent when she awoke. Since Alek had ripped her shirt the night before, she thought it only fair he replaced it. She took the tunic meant for him. The way she saw it—a shirt for a shirt. Dresses were not her style. Skirts were impractical on a fueling dock. At any time she could be called to run the pumps or crawl into a maintenance hatch, or forced to run the lengths of the docks to scoop up her drunken father before he gambled away something they couldn't live without.

Darkness was gone, replaced by a soft green haze of light. To the left of the tent-filled valley, a colossal forest stretched into the distance. The green, overlarge leaves had begun to expand now that daylight had returned to them. Their night of rest was over. The trees towered high above the planet's surface, thicker than some of the smaller spacecrafts that landed on her fueling dock home. She'd been lost in those trees? What had she been thinking, running off in the dark into that thick wilderness? She was lucky it was Alek who'd found her and not some wild beast.

"My lady?" The servant who had been carrying the clothes paused in his return journey. He looked at her expectantly. Kendall shook her head in denial and pulled the flap down over her face. She waited several minutes before looking out again. The servant was gone.

It was early. The Galaxy Brides' ship might still be in orbit. She poked at her hand. She couldn't go back to the ship. They would know who she was and would make her marry someone, if not here, then on the next stop. She might not get another chance to get away. Thanks to Alek, they believed her contractual duty was done. She wondered how exactly the Qurilixian men paid for brides—by potential shipment or by units kept. Would Alek have to pay for her even if she didn't stay? She swallowed down her guilt. She would just have to find a way to pay him back no matter the cost.

"Where are you going?" Alek asked, jarring her from her thoughts. He didn't sound sleepy. She turned to see his clear eyes studying her and wondered how long he'd been awake.

"Nowhere, for now," she answered. "I didn't mean to wake you. I was trying to be quiet."

"You didn't. I heard the servant come by to drop off our clothing this morning."

"But..." She looked down at the tunic she wore. "Why didn't you say anything?"

His lips pulled up into a mischievous grin. "It was adorable to watch you sneak around." Then, lifting a brow, he added, "Especially when you climbed out of bed naked."

She gave a small laugh and looked back outside the tent. Tiny particles of dust danced in the sunlight. She watched them drift aimlessly. They reminded her of the old air vent she and Margot had turned into a fort. The cleaning droids couldn't get into the space, and when the sisters had climbed in and stirred the dust, it had danced in the artificial light streaming through the old grate. For a moment, the sound of Margot's giggle echoed inside her mind. A wave of pain and worry washed over her heart.

"I am going to need my shirt back before we finish the ceremony," Alek said. She heard him move off the bed. When she drew her gaze from the dust-stirred memory, she found he was almost to the food table. He glanced over it, absently plucking one of the chocolates off the pile and tossing it into his mouth as if it were nothing special. She eyed the treat, wanting a piece but unwilling to take one of the expensive morsels. Kendall knew there was no way a man like Alek could afford it—especially if he couldn't afford to lend her the passage fare home.

He was naked from the night before. In the soft daylight she could make out every detail of him perfectly. His dark hair was tousled. It added an intimate, sleepy beauty to the scene. His muscles flexed, drawing attention to his back. The shallow valley of his spine cut a path downward, encouraging her eyes to the very firm cheeks of his ass.

"Is the chocolate provided by the planet's royalty?" Kendall's throat was dry. She forced her gaze away from his ass to the tent wall. The harder she tried not to look, the more she found her eyes glancing in his direction.

His expression was quizzical when he looked back at her. "No. It's part of our trade agreements. The monks use a lot of fuel ore to travel the universes on their missionary tours. I suppose one of my brother's servants ordered it. I actually never thought to ask."

"I see." Kendall swallowed, a little unnerved as to where she was supposed to turn her gaze. It was one thing to be next to him in the haze of darkness and desire, quite another to watch him move about naked as if flesh was his every day attire. As his body angled to the side showing the proud glory of his manhood nestled between his thighs, she again turned her attention to the tent wall.

"What is it?" Alek crossed toward her but stopped when she pulled her arms closer to her sides. It was a little hard to concentrate when he looked the way he did. She wondered if he was even aware of it. Then, thinking of the fact they wore loincloths in hopes of having a marital cere-mony, she doubted he cared.

"Kendall?"

"You don't think I am good to my word. That is why you refused to lend me the passage fare to my home." The idea made her sad, though she could understand it. Despite the fun they'd had, they were essentially strangers.

"I have no reason to doubt your word."

Kendall let her lids shade her eyes as she glanced to the side. His cock had lifted some. She tugged at the hem of her borrowed shirt. "Ah, forgive me. I assumed you had access to family money to afford chocolate and servants. I shouldn't have jumped to conclusions. It was very rude of me." She absently touched her hand, rubbing at it to find the tracker. Her skin itched the more she thought about the device in there. "I'm just desperate to find my way home."

"The gods would not send me someone who was not worthy," he said. "Your home is with me now."

"That is a nice offer, Alek, but I can't stay here. I'm sorry." She gave him a weak smile. Last night had been enjoyable, but she had to get home to her sister.

"It wasn't an offer so much as a fact. After last night, honor demands that you stay with me." He glanced at the bed. "What we did—"

"You want to have a long-term relationship after one night of a little messing around?" She tried not to laugh in surprise. Most men she knew ran from commitment—especially after they got what they wanted from a woman. At least, that was the impression she'd always gotten off the men she observed interacting with fellow travelers at the fueling dock.

"You removed my mask," he said seriously. "Custom dictates that—"

"No, you took off your own mask and tossed it at me." It was then she realized he'd been looking at the mask on the bed and not the bed itself. Her eyes again darted to his waist before finding the tent wall.

She waited for an answer, but it didn't come. Out of the corner of her eye she saw Alek turn his back to her. She let loose a captured breath and watched his backside as he moved. It was really hard to concentrate when he was naked.

"Transport off the planet will be difficult." Alek's words were low and steady. "We do not allow many visitors in our air space. Even fewer are allowed to land."

"I understand, but you see I have to figure something out," she insisted. "I can't remain here."

He fingered the wine pitcher before pouring a goblet. "My brother Mirek, Ealdorman of Draig, is the mining ambassador. His work takes him to space to meet with the visiting dignitaries. He would know who could be trusted to take you off world."

"Thank you, Alek." She took an anxious step toward him. "You have done so much for me in this very short time, more than anyone I can remember in my whole life. I will repay the passage. I am—"

"There is a condition."

"Condition?" She stopped, worried by the sudden businesslike tone of his voice.

"Yes." He traced the lip of the goblet, concentrating on it more than was necessary. "All know you have spent the night in here with me. I'll be honest. My family has not had the best of luck when it comes to finding wives. If I go out there and tell them I failed to prove my worth to you as a husband, my family name, my personal honor, will be disgraced."

"I didn't mean to cause you problems," she said. "I never meant to disgrace you. I just can't marry you."

"I understand." He shot her a stern look, cutting her off from saying more. "However, my people will not understand. To us, this marriage is willed by the gods. So here is my proposal. You cannot find passage off this planet for some time. There is nothing to be done about that. We can't force ships to come to our airspace and meetings were not scheduled this close to the yearly ceremony since it was hoped Mirek would find a bride and would be otherwise occupied with a wife. You also have no method of sustaining yourself in the meantime. You have no place to live. After seeing your fear in the forest last night, I do not recommend you trying to survive on your own. I, in good conscience, could not allow it."

"You said you have a condition for helping me?"

"Marry me. Finish the ceremony today. Smile." He paused, again concentrating on the cup's lip. "Pretend to be happy as I present you before my people. Later today, we will leave the ceremony grounds for my home. I will speak with Mirek about finding you a safe ride off world just as soon as we arrive. I cannot promise it will be fast. I do not know how long it will be until a suitable transport is found, but if you help me with my family's honor, I will help you."

His proposal made sense, for both of them. But then why did it leave her feeling cold and empty inside? A business marriage? She knew such things were done. They would both benefit from the arrangement. It should have been a simple answer. However, this was not a simple situation.

"What do I have to do to finish the ceremony?" She traced her hand, digging so hard it hurt. Still she didn't feel the embedded tracker.

"It's quite simple, my lady," Alek said evenly as he lifted the goblet to his lips. He took a drink. "All you have to do is break a stone."

Simple?

Alek would have laughed it he didn't feel so terrible. There was nothing simple about his proposal. It took all his willpower to get the words out. But what else could he do? She was right. He'd removed his own mask. She had accepted nothing. She hadn't asked to be his wife. He'd just assumed. When she'd moved against him in the night, whispering his name, climaxing against his body, he'd thought she felt the connection between them.

How could she not feel it?

If he couldn't keep his destined mate, what good was he? How could he face his people, his brothers, with a failed marriage attempt and a glowing crystal? It would be much better to find an excuse later to explain her absence, after Kendall showed she chose to be with him. Perhaps she would be called to her home world. It wasn't far from the truth. She did seek to go home. Later, he could go into mourning and let people believe she'd died. It wouldn't be hard to convince them without saying a word, so technically it wouldn't be lying. People always accused him of not speaking of his emotions anyway. No one would expect him to talk about it. He was sure the pain of her loss would show on him. Only two of them would know the truth. He would never tell and she would never return.

Alek swallowed down his pain. He eyed his glowing crystal and then the raised platform where the king and queen waited to bless the marriages as they were announced. His tunic shirt smelled of her. It was sweet intoxication at its most torturous. He'd ordered his loosely fitting black pants, dark-blue tunic shirt and a matching gown for his bride years ago when he'd come to his first ceremony. He had nearly forgotten what they looked like.

Like most Draig ceremonies, the crystal breaking would be short. He was glad for it. Alek would not be able to stand before the council of elders and his royal aunt and uncle for too long. He was sure they would sense his pain.

"Lord Alek!"

Alek stopped on his way to the platform, frowning at the panicked young voice. Rey lived near the mountain castle and often ran errands for Cenek. Like most boys his age, he was well trained in the mountain routes and could navigate his way to the palace from the mountain fortress without help.

"Easy, boy," Alek said. "You look as if you have been running all night. What is it?"

"Master Cenek sent me to give you this." The boy handed the missive over while his eyes strayed to Kendall in curiosity. "The ceffyl colt did not make it."

Rey's words repeated what Cenek said inside the missive, only Cenek provided more detail. The mare had given birth to a stillborn baby. It had been quick and unpreventable. The mother lived and was fine, if not a bit despondent after the event. Cenek bid Alek to stay as long as he wished at the palace. What could be done had been done.

"Master Cenek said I was to give it to you straight away.'" The boy again looked at Kendall. It became evident that Cenek, despite his encouragement, did not think Alek would be too occupied this morning.

"You've done well," Alek said, shoving the missive into the waistband of his pants beneath the long tunic shirt. He would dispose of it later. With the colt dead, there wasn't anything for him to do at the moment. However, the fact that some of the older generations considered a stillborn animal to be a bad omen was not lost on him. That he'd found out about it seconds before he finalized his marriage was something he refused to think about. There was no turning back now. This was his course. "Find refreshments before you return, and stay out of the palace stables. I do not want another report of the ceffyl tags being rearranged. Whoever did it is lucky they were not caught for the prank."

Rey grinned and jogged away with the aimless

energy only kids possessed. It had been a harmless prank, but one that took some sorting since the tags identified the diets and quirks of the different animals.

"He travels alone?" Kendall asked, watching the boy. "Is that safe? Should he wait and travel with us?"

Alek frowned. "He is fifteen years and knows the mountain terrain as well as any adult."

Kendall looked unconvinced.

The king and queen sat on their thrones in royal purple. Crowns adorned their heads. As Alek approached, they motioned him to come forward with his bride. Queen Mede was a rare Qurilixian-born woman, but that was not how she came to be married to the king. Their match had been fated just as everyone else's was.

"Queen Mede, King Llyr, may I present my wife, Lady Kendall Haven," Alek said.

Kendall smiled and bowed her head exactly like he'd told her to. "Queen Mede, King Llyr, it is a great honor."

"Proceed," the queen ordered.

Kendall turned to Alek. Her eyes stared into his, seeming to ask him if he was sure about this course of action. Closing his eyes, he bowed his head forward so she could remove the crystal from his neck. He felt the absence of its light weight. She dropped it on the ground and pressed her foot on top of it. A moment passed and she glanced up at him. Taking his arm, her plastered smile faltered and she seemed to struggle. Alek glanced down, seeing the glow coming from beneath her foot.

"It won't break," she whispered almost desperately. Usually, the rocks shattered easily. Her fingers tightened on his arm as she twisted her toes. Alek did the only thing he could think of. He stepped on the top of her foot and pressed down. She flinched. The stone cracked and popped, its light fading. They both stepped back to see the broken stone.

Cheering erupted from the gathered crowd. The queen announced, "Welcome to the family of Draig, Lady Kendall. I hope you will enjoy your new home."

Kendall gave Alek a relieved smile. For a moment, he could almost believe the look was for him, that the happiness he imagined in her eyes was real. Alek took her arm and led her from the platform back toward the tents.

When they were out of sight of the royals, she let loose a big sigh. "There is something to be said for your quick marital ceremonies—a few words, a few nods and it's all over. Though, I didn't think the crystal was going to be that hard to break."

"Come on," he said, not liking the easy way she talked about the little show they had just put on. By breaking his crystal, his fate was sealed. Either he made a marriage with Kendall work, or he would be forever alone. There was no second chance for his kind. This was it. Kendall would be his only bride.

Then I will have to convince her to stay, he told himself. *I must make her choose me.*

A plan formed in his head. He had given his word that he'd help her find a transport after they arrived at his home and he spoke to Mirek. What if he took a long route to his home? It was not as if duty called him back. With the news of the lost colt, there would be no work for him to attend to— at least nothing that could not wait. He could travel around the mountain paths and valleys for days, months even. If he timed it right, Mirek would be gone when he arrived. That would give him more time. Kendall could come to see what he already knew. They were willed by the gods to be together. They were destined.

"Why are you looking at me like that?" Kendall asked, eyeing him warily. "Did I not perform the ceremony right? I really did try to break the crystal, but it was hard to crack."

"It's done. We're married," he answered. "That is all that matters right now."

5

"I DIDN'T SAY anything before, but I am sorry about your loss."

Alek didn't look up from where he stroked the ceffyl's neck. Checking the mount was automatic for him. As the Top Breeder, he had been responsible for the animal's birth and training. The creatures all remembered him as the first human they'd imprinted to. Ever since he was a boy, he'd had a natural ability with all animals. Even in shifted form, he could get closer than any of his brothers or friends.

"There is not much to be done about it. The crystal needed to be broken for the ceremony." He looked into the ceffyl's eyes. The creature hissed, extending her long, thin tongue. It hit his chest affectionately before she retracted it. Alek didn't want to think about the crystal, or his wife's desire to leave. He would focus instead on convincing her to stay.

"I meant the colt," Kendall clarified. "I saw your expression when the boy told you. The news affected you greatly."

"The animal was my responsibility. Had I been there, it is possible he would be alive. Instead, I had other duties to attend to."

"The ceremony?" she asked perceptively.

He nodded once, not wanting to discuss it further. Turning his attention to the nearby stableman, he said, "She's gotten into a patch of solar flowers. Do not let her eat for two days or she'll be sick. And I don't care how pitiful she looks. Those flowers need to digest fully." Then, as he studied the animal, he added as an afterthought, "I would not inform Queen Mede. I imagine there is a missing patch of flowers somewhere in her garden. I would check the grazing pen to make sure they're not escaping from it somehow."

The stableman nodded, quirking the smallest of amused smiles. "I'll take care of it, my lord." He led the beast toward the back of the royal stables to isolate her from the rest of the stock. Ceffyls loved to eat just about as much as they liked to sleep. The beast would not be happy to go without food for two days, even though she could last months without sustenance.

Alek began to walk the length of the stables, moving from stall to stall to check on the animals. Those working acknowledged him but went about their business. Their eyes strayed to the new lady at his side, though they did not speak to her.

"You're very important, aren't you?" Kendall whispered, as if she were divulging some secret. She held herself back from the animals, keeping a wary eye on them as if she expected the beasts to break through their stalls and attack. Her demeanor made a few of the animals uneasy as they sensed her fear of them.

He wasn't sure how to answer without sounding conceited. "My family is, yes. As the nephews of the king, we are one of the premier houses on the planet."

"That is why you were worried about the marriage thing," she said, as if it now just made sense to her.

They might not be standing close, but the stablemen could easily listen to what was being said. Not liking the fact she spoke about such things within earshot of the others, he announced, "We will take this one." Alek patted a particularly large and somewhat temperamental ceffyl. The beast would cause him problems, but he was not in a hurry to get home. The stableman hesitated at the choice but didn't question it as he got the steed ready.

"Do you require food before we leave?" he asked, leading Kendall out of the stables into the sunlight. "My uncle has invited us to the palace."

The Draig palace, much like his home, was made to be a fortress. From the ground, because of the angle, it was impossible to see the windows or balconies that adjoined to the royal family quarters on the upper levels. They were carved so that even from a distance it looked like a mountain cliff. Within the surrounding valley, near the festival grounds, a small village was nestled under the protection of the House of Draig. The roads were of rocky earth, smoothed flat and even. The village was kept immaculately clean, built with almost a military perfection of angles. The houses were of rock and wood, so that even the poorest of families were well provided for.

"Your uncle the king? I suppose we cannot refuse such an invitation, but…" She looked at the two guards at the mountain's base. They protected the entrance to the palace.

When they were several yards away from the stables, he stopped. "But?"

"Please, don't make me. It was hard enough standing in front of all those people to finish the ceremony. Do you really want me to embarrass you by not knowing your royal dining customs?"

She had a point. He didn't really want to expose their marriage to more scrutiny. "It will be as you wish. Honor demanded I extend the offer to you. I'll politely decline."

"Thank you, Alek." She sighed in relief. For a moment, he almost returned her slight smile, until she added, "Besides, I really think we should leave. It's already late in the day and the sooner we go, the sooner we will get where we are going. I need to find a way off planet, the sooner the better."

THE CEFFYL ROCKED BACK and forth, each step cumbersome and, frankly, a little angry. Kendall stared at the center horn on the beast's head, watching it twitch and sway, waiting for a sign the animal would thrust its head back and stab her in the stomach for daring to ride it. Why did Alek have to pick this animal with so many others in the stables? Its horn was much longer and much sharper than the other creatures. In fact, the longer she stared at it, the more certain she became that the horn was growing sharper by the second.

"You will not be as sore later if you relax into the gait of the beast instead of fighting it," Alek said behind her. At first, his hands had been on her hips, holding her upright. Now, he barely touched her. Her rigid posture put space between their bodies, though she could still feel the warmth of him against her back.

They were on a wide red-gray path. Mountain peaks spread out over the distance, forming a surreal view with their jagged tops piercing the green-tinted sky. From their vantage point on the path, she could see well into the distance. There was so much space, so many places for wild things to hide. The higher up the mountain they rode, the grayer the earth became until there was no red tint left.

Kendall took a deep breath, not sure why exactly she was having a hard time breathing. She suspected it was a combination of the ugly beast beneath her and the incredibly sexy beast behind her. As her focus shifted more to the man in back, she noticed the brush of his thigh rocking along her hip.

"Relax." He slipped his hand onto her side. Fingers curled around her waist, letting her feel the natural rhythm of the ceffyl. She closed her eyes, no longer concerned with being impaled—at least not by the animal. The passion she'd shared with Alek but had been unable to fully consummate worked its spell over them once more.

With each movement of the animal, she slipped back by a small degree. His hand stayed firm, not pulling, merely guiding her to him. Thighs lightly touched the backs of her legs, only to press more insistently with each stride. She slid against the unmistakable lift of his arousal. He rolled his hips, thrusting forward in a fluid motion. There was purpose in his caress. She closed her eyes, letting her head fall back against his chest. The fingers along her waist spread wide over her stomach.

Alek moved his mouth to her ear. The whisper of his breath tickled her skin seconds before he flicked his tongue against a sensitive lobe. "Now that it is day, there is no reason we cannot finish what we were doing last night."

Kendall shivered at the feel of him moving his lips softly down the back of her neck. He pushed her hair to the side for better access. A throaty moan reverberated against her flesh. Alek lifted his hand from her stomach to her jaw, angling her chin. He placed gentle kisses along her nape, moving as if the simple act was the most important thing in the universe. He pulled at her gown and soon her bodice was loosened. His hips rocked into her. When he uncovered a breast, he massaged his fingers over a peaked nipple.

Kendall reached for his leg. She kneaded the thick muscle she found there. Everything inside her focused on him—his warmth, his smell, his kiss, his touch. Their bodies rocked, steadily moving back and forth as the animal lumbered forward.

"Turn around," he whispered.

At the request, her eyes flew open, back to the center horn. The animal had begun to jerk its head forcefully to each side. "I think your animal needs to rest. It looks agitated."

Alek lifted his head to look at the beast. "Perhaps you are right."

Before she could speak, he dismounted and was pulling her against his chest. He turned her, putting his back to the ceffyl as his lips met hers. A stiff breeze swept up the mountain, encasing them. Her skirt billowed around the backs of her thighs. Alek enticed her tongue into his mouth.

Kendall traced the length of his arms beneath his tunic shirt, holding him to her. She liked the taste of him, the wet texture of his open mouth. He seemed to touch everywhere at once—her hair, back, arms, hip and ass—before working the skirt material at her waist. He exposed her calf, inching the dress higher even as he continued to kiss her.

With each second, he kissed harder. Alek reached for his waist, eagerly trying to remove the barriers between their bodies. She felt his hand bump against her sex. What was it about this man that could make her forget everything but the very basest of needs? Before last night, she never would have believed herself capable of such passion. Sure, she had needs before Alek, but nothing she couldn't take care of on her own.

She reached for him, intent on rubbing against him as they had the night before. Swaying, she was held up only by his embrace. A throaty laugh left him, vibrating against her mouth. She smiled into his kiss as he pulled back to look at her.

"Oh! Ah!" For a moment, the sound didn't fully register. She looked at his mouth, but his lips hadn't moved to release the feminine, higher-toned squeal of alarm. Reason dawned in his eyes as they both turned their heads to the side. She recognized Aeron from the Galaxy Brides' ship. The woman stared at them, her eyes wide as she said, "I... Apologies... Walking..."

Kendall looked at Alek's face and then down his body to where her hand gripped him in an intimate manner. Embarrassment heated her face as she let go of his arousal. His hands were much slower in releasing their hold on her. When he finally let her go, Kendall swept her hands over her body to make sure she was covered.

"I didn't mean to intrude," Aeron said, clearly regaining her senses. "I've been walking for a long time."

"Who are you?" Alek questioned. "What are you doing with that ceffyl?"

Aeron glanced behind her to the animal following her over the ridge. The smaller ceffyl lowered its head and moved toward Alek's surly beast. The two of them began rubbing horns. Alek seemed unconcerned with the animals' ritual.

"It followed me," Aeron answered. She looked almost desperately at Kendall for help. The woman wasn't a friend, but Alek's harsh tone had clearly frightened the poor thing. Kendal felt sorry for her.

"Alek, this is Aeron. She was on the Galaxy Brides' ship with me," Kendall explained. She tried not to look directly at Alek for too long. Her body still stung with the disappointment of the interruption. However, perhaps it was better they didn't continue. She should consider what she was doing logically, not in the heat of his kisses.

"Aeron Grey," Aeron said, belatedly.

"What are you doing out here alone, Aeron Grey?" Alek asked.

The woman looked as if she might cry. She shook her head back and forth. "I don't know."

"Where is your husband?" Alek took an aggressive step toward Aeron. Kendall watched his actions closely, unsure what to make of his hard attitude. It was obvious by the woman's expression that she was frightened. She was alone in the wilderness on a new planet. Shouldn't the question have been, "Are you all right?" Not, "Where is your husband?"

"I'm not really married. I mean, I am, but I'm not. It's hard to explain," Aeron said.

Alek shot a sidelong glance to his wife and mumbled under his breath about how there seemed to be a lot of complications with the current bridal shipment.

Kendall looked to the ground, not liking his harsh tone especially now that it was directed at her. She took a step away from him toward Aeron, putting herself between the two of them to diffuse the tense situation. To Aeron, she questioned, "What happened?"

"I don't know. There was the ceremony and then the king drugged me with this yellow pollen thing and then I was taken to…" Aeron turned and pointed up the mountain, clearly flustered and not making a lot of sense, "…to this cabin home in the mountains. I took a bath, went to bed and I woke up alone."

Alek took another forceful step in a clear effort to intimidate Aeron, which wasn't necessary considering the poor woman already looked unnerved. "The mountain cabin? What happened? Where is your husband?"

"I…" Aeron stumbled back. Alek grabbed the

woman's arm and jerked her to stand before him. He gave her a rough shake and forced her to stay upright when she swayed. Panicked, Aeron said, "I don't know."

"What have you done?" he demanded.

"I did nothing!" she yelled. "I woke up and he was gone."

"Who?"

"My husband," she answered, desperately tugging at her arm. "I waited for him for hours, most of the day, but I think he must have gone out the night before and he didn't come back. He didn't say what he was doing. I tried to find him, but it was as if he was just snatched from the ground into the heavens. I couldn't even see footprints."

Kendall watched, unsure what to do. From what she could guess by the time that had passed and the haze of light, it was late in the day. Aeron had been at the bridal ceremony the night before. Kendall wondered if the woman was drugged, or perhaps simply confused by the daylight.

Every muscle in Alek's body was rigid. Surely this wasn't a reaction to being interrupted during sex, before completion? She waited breathlessly, staring at his hand on Aeron's arm. No, this was something more. Why was it this man had come to her rescue like a chivalrous gentleman and was now treating Aeron like some kind of alien invader?

"Who is your husband?" Alek demanded more than asked.

"B—Bron," she stammered. "He's the High—"

"I know who he is," Alek snapped. He let go of Aeron's arm. He looked at Kendall and then Aeron. "We must go to the cabin. Bron would not have left her alone. Not for so long. Something must have happened." He looked suspiciously at Aeron. "Or someone did something to him."

"I—"

His look stopped Aeron from finishing. "We ride to the cabin," Alek ordered.

Kendall frowned, not liking his high-handed way. "What about your home? We were going—"

"Our home will have to wait," he broke in. "Get on the ceffyl."

Aeron moved, slow to obey as she went to the smaller animal.

Kendall didn't readily follow his command. She crossed her arms and gave him a stern look. This was not the Alek from the night before, the man who had saved her from the trackers, the man who smiled at her and kissed her. This Alek was hard and frankly a little mean. She didn't appreciate this side of him.

"Get on the ceffyl," he repeated, directing the

command at her. There was a stubbornness in his expression, demanding to be obeyed without question. Not even her father dared to order her around like that. In fact, she'd been in charge of her own life since she could remember—not counting the whole repossession ordeal.

Kendall shivered as anger started to unfurl inside her chest, and still she didn't move. He narrowed his eyes. She tried to keep his churning gaze but found herself looking away first. Strong emotions boiled beneath his surface, held back by the hard shell of his exterior. She tried to stand her ground, but he won. This was a strange land and she was at his mercy for the time being. Even in her irritation, she was rational enough to realize that much. She kept her distance as she moved past him to go to the large beast. The giant animal didn't seem so fearsome now compared to Alex's liquid-gold expression.

She felt more than saw Alek behind her. He touched her waist and she tensed.

"I did not mean to speak so harshly. He is my brother, Kendall," Alek said softly. "He would not disappear on his new bride. Something must have happened to him. I must find him."

Kendall nodded, sensing more than seeing his concern. Her anger faded as fast as it had risen. Sibling worry was something she understood all too well. Her own worry for her sister filled her. She allowed Alek to help her onto the animal. He took his place in front of her, forcing her to hold on to his waist. Soon the ceffyls were running at a hard, fast pace. They traveled in relative silence. Only once did Aeron speak, venturing to ask Kendall if she'd seen Riona Grey, Aeron's sister. Apparently, the woman had left without saying goodbye to Aeron. Kendall knew enough about Riona to not be surprised. Riona was a known gambler and had made no attempt to hide her profession. Kendall couldn't respect the woman, not after what her own gambling father had done to her. Some said gaming was a disease. Kendall didn't care what those some called it. Gambling had ruined her life. It had been all she could do growing up to keep the fueling station in one piece, and her father away from the gaming chips. Even with her diligence, she'd clearly failed to watch him at all hours of the day. She told Aeron everything she knew about Riona's whereabouts, which was absolutely nothing.

The path suddenly ended in a steep incline. Alek leaned forward. Kendall held on tightly as the animal began to climb. It quickly zigzagged up the small cliff. The ground leveled but she didn't loosen her hold until Alek tapped her gripping fingers. Aeron's animal followed closely behind them.

A long building stood back from the edge of the cliff nestled into dense underbrush with a dirt path leading around the side. Unlike the forest by the ceremonial grounds, the trees here were skinny with thick, willowy tops. Behind her, the view stretched for miles. It only proved how out of her element she was. This world was nothing but open spaces and wilderness dotted with tiny signs of civilization.

The building was constructed from blocks of precisely cut gray stone and topped with a flat roof. A single plank of wood made the oversized door, the grain spiraling from the middle. Most likely, the wood came from the forest near the palace. There didn't seem to be any trees that thick in the mountains.

Alek swung off the mount and held his hand to Kendall to help her down. The ceffyl stretched out on the ground, resting lazily as he licked at the thin slivers of gray-blue grass. The beast twirled his tongue around the stalks before pulling the blades into his mouth. A low hissing noise sounded as he chewed.

Kendall turned to follow the others but kept her eyes on the beast. Her inattention caused her to trip on a bag Aeron had dropped on the ground. Alek automatically grabbed her arm, steadying her. She shivered a little at his touch, but he didn't seem to notice as he looked over the clearing.

"I'll see if he returned while I was gone." Aeron said from the cabin door.

Alek lifted his head and inhaled deeply. He let go of Kendall's arm. "No. He's not here." His eyes shifted to gold. "I detect his scent in the forest, but it is faint, hours old."

"You can tell that just by smelling?" Kendall asked, surprised.

Alek nodded absently. He gazed down the path they'd traveled, focusing intently. "Go inside. Stay here together. Do not leave the house. I go to look for my brother."

"Alek?" Kendall shook her head in protest. He couldn't just leave her in the middle of the wilderness. She might know who Aeron was, but she didn't really *know* the woman. It's not like she'd talked to the other women on the spaceship. The fact Alek seemed worried about something happening to his brother did nothing to ease her fears. There was no telling what lurked out there in the wilds of Qurilixen.

"It will be fine," he said. For the briefest of moments, his eyes softened. "The cabin is safe. I will come back."

"How can you know that?" she tried to ask, but the words barely slipped past her tightening throat.

Then it was too late to say anything. Alek shifted, his body hardening as he turned his attention to the mountain forest. The form of the dragon came over him, from the talons on his fingertips to the hard ridge along his forehead. He surged forward and disappeared into a blur within the trees.

Aeron made a weak noise and Kendall turned her attention to the cabin. She couldn't decide what to do, unsure what to make of her situation. She should have been relishing in her freedom from captivity, but this place hardly seemed free. Sure, there were wide open spaces, but where in the world was she supposed to run to? In many ways on world was more of a prison than those tiny crates they'd stuffed her in.

"Don't be scared," Kendall said, trying to push through her own fear. "The Galaxy Brides' downloads were somewhat incomplete. These men are shifters."

Aeron nodded. "I know. Bron showed me." She quickly turned toward the door and reached above her head. She placed her hand against the middle stone. Seconds later, the door unlatched. She hooked the side with her finger and pulled it open. "If I looked worried it was because I couldn't help wondering what we would do if Alek does not come back."

Kendall gazed to where Alek had disappeared

into the forest. Her heart beat hard in her chest. Why did Aeron have to say the words out loud? Fear curled inside her. Fear for her safety. Fear for Alek. She might not plan on staying married to the man, but he had saved her from the men trying to reclaim her as property. Plus, he had given her the tracking device instead of keeping it for himself.

"It was just a worry. I'm sure he will return. He seems very taken with you." Aeron smiled, but the look was forced. "I'm just glad someone else is here to look for him. I didn't know what to do. I don't know anything about these forests, let alone track-ing. I'm not even sure how to get back to the palace. I was guessing."

When Aeron moved to go inside, Kendall had little choice but to follow. She looked up as she passed under the hand scanner, but the unit wasn't noticeable. Sunlight streamed inside the narrow window. It reflected off a rectangular mirror mounted on a tall column and then onto other strategically placed mirrors higher on the walls to bathe the cabin's interior with light. The entryway led to one large room with three arched doorways. The walls and floor were stone, built from the same kind of precisely cut blocks as the exterior. There wasn't much by the way of décor beyond the fine craftsmanship of the structure. A large, dormant fire pit stood barren in the middle of the room. A domed hood was placed high above it, leading up a long column to the ceiling to filter out the smoke.

Cushioned furniture surrounded the fire pit. The bases were a combination of stone and wood. A long polished stone table stood at the far side of the room, large enough to seat a dozen people. Bench seating curved around its oval shape.

Kendall automatically followed as Aeron led the way to a food-preparation area. She watched curiously as the other woman busied herself cooking. Of course Kendall knew some planets still prepared food by hand, but she'd never actually seen the process done. Most of her meals came from her personal food simulator in her office or the small diner in the fueling dock.

Aeron gave her a curious look but said nothing. The silence between them began to feel oppressive. If anything, life on the fueling dock had taught her the art of quick conversations. "You said you're not really married? If you don't plan on being married, why did you get on the ship?"

"It's a long story," Aeron answered. "And you? You seemed pretty comfortable with your husband, yet he appeared to be unconvinced of your plans to be his wife."

"It's a long story," Kendall said. It wasn't something she wanted to discuss. She thought of her sister. She had to get back home before her father gambled away the girl. Margot wouldn't be able to defend herself. She was a pretty child. Some men paid big money for pretty children. The universe was a very large and ugly place. Kendall counted herself lucky to have been dropped off on a respectable planet. These men wanted women for marriage and treated them well enough—or at least that was the case from what she'd witnessed so far.

Aeron gave a wry laugh and mumbled, "Fair answer."

"Alek has his appeal," Kendall explained in an effort to be friendlier, "and he did me a great favor, which makes me indebted to him, but I have a family matter that requires I leave."

Aeron paused in what she was doing. "And if you could stay, would you?"

Kendall gestured helplessly before picking up a piece of hard, round vegetable. She studied it instead of meeting the other woman's gaze. "I don't know."

How could she answer that? Staying would be insane, wouldn't it? She'd just met Alek. This wasn't her home world. These weren't her people. Sure, the idea of seeing the mining process up close and personal held some appeal, but was that academic interest enough to justify a life with one man? Why was she even considering it? There wasn't a choice. She had to find her sister. It wouldn't do her any good to ponder things that couldn't be realized.

"Bron has his appeal, as well," Aeron said, "when he's not speaking to me as if I am to be ordered about like a servant."

"Must be a family trait," Kendall mumbled, thinking of how Alek had ordered her onto the ceffyl. She smiled and made her way into the kitchen. She liked Aeron, despite the standoffish demeanor the woman sometimes presented. "Can I help with something?"

Aeron handed her a knife. "Can you use this?"

Kendall looked at the weapon, lifted her arm and aimed at a far post in the living room. The blade wobbled between her fingers. "I was shown once, but…"

Aeron chuckled and pulled at Kendall's wrist to keep her from throwing it. "For cutting the meat." The woman showed her how to use the blade to make incisions in the meat. The raw food was cold to the touch and had a very strange texture. She tried not to think about what she was touching as she cut it into thin strips.

Aeron put water into a pot and put it over an open flame. "I don't know what I was expecting when I first heard about this planet, but these men were not it. I expected, well, I think I expected a bunch of primordial grunting and using aggressive signs to communicate."

Kendall burst into laughter, unable to help it.

"Horrible of me, right?"

"No," Kendall shook her head. "Those Galaxy Brides uploads left a lot to be desired. Half of the information seems antiquated and the other half is just wrong. They didn't mention anything about this being a planet of shifters. I nearly messed myself when I saw Alek coming for me in the dark forest. I thought I was about to get eaten alive."

"Oh, that ship." Aeron shook her head. "Some of those women!"

At the same time, both women said, "Gina."

"I've never seen a woman so proud over her oversized, unnatural…" Kendall gestured her hands in front of her chest.

"Torpedo missiles?" Aeron supplied.

"They're probably just as deadly."

Aeron snorted. "More so, I'd wager, and hard as rocks."

"I grew up on a fueling dock." Kendall finished cutting one piece of meat and began on the next one. She thought it best to turn the subject away from wagers and bets. She didn't know how much Aeron was like her sister, Riona the gambler. "I'm used to a variety of aliens, just not the wide open spaces."

"I worked in a small metal room," Aeron said. The water had started to boil and the woman dropped vegetables into it. A pale piece caused steam to hiss from the pot. Aeron snapped her hand back with a small gasp of surprise. Shaking the limb a couple times, she resumed the process with more care. "I'm not used to interacting with aliens or wide open spaces. In fact, I'm not used to conversations that don't include a communicator."

"So, why were you on the Galaxy Brides' ship?"

"It really is a long story. I needed to secure a meeting on this planet and my sister…" Aeron paused in thought before finishing. "My sister was in charge of the travel arrangements. She's a little unconventional when it comes to such things. To tell the truth, she's unconventional when it comes to most things."

Kendall followed Aeron's gaze to where she stared at the front door. "I would tell you that he's fine, but I have no way of knowing if that is true."

Aeron cleared her throat and went back to work with a renewed force. She took the meat strips and laid them out over the cooking fire. "Thank you for the thought. I honestly don't know why I'm worried. This is their homeland. He probably just lost track of time, or was distracted by something important."

"I'm sure that's it," Kendall said, though she

wasn't convinced. The strange smell coming from the sizzling pan caught her attention and she stepped back, wrinkling her nose. "Is meat supposed to smell like that?"

"Only when it doesn't come from a simulator," Aeron answered.

Kendall tried not to breathe. Her stomach churned.

"You look a little pale. Why don't you wait in the other room? I'll finish up. Explore the cabin if you like. I don't think anyone will care."

Grateful for an excuse to leave the suddenly potent smell in the kitchen, she wandered around the cabin. She peeked out of the windows, trying to see Alek in the narrow views. He wasn't there. A bathing room was close to the front door. It contained a water bath instead of a laser decontaminator. The fact wasn't surprising. A doorway at the far end of the cabin led to a series of sleeping rooms. Each one had a bed and some sort of wardrobe or trunk. There were twelve in total. Only the one at the very end of the hall looked as if it had been slept in recently. It was the largest and by far the most comfortable looking.

With so many vacant rooms, the cabin felt particularly empty. She tried not to think of the forest beyond the cabin, the miles upon miles of landscape. Instead, she thought of the stars, the inky black of the high skies as seen through her fueling dock window. Was Margot in her room even now, going through Kendall's things, looking for a clue, worried? Would their father even tell the child what had happened or would he be too ashamed? Her father was a weak man. There was no way he would admit to it. What if Margot thought Kendall abandoned her?

"Ah, my poor sister. Don't believe it. Please don't believe it. I would never abandon you. You have to know that." Kendall tried to push down her anxiety. The whispered words did little to comfort her. How long had it been? Weeks? No, it was most likely months. It was hard to tell when they'd drugged her and transported her like merchandise.

"Kendall?" Aeron's voice called. "The food is ready if you are hungry."

"What do I do?" she whispered.

"Kendall?" Aeron yelled louder.

"Coming!" Kendall followed the sound of Aeron's voice. There were no answers anyone could give her, not on this planet.

6

ALEK USED every sense he had to detect Bron in the forest. It was nearly impossible. His brother's scent was faint and he lost it several times.

Bron would not leave his bride, so something had to be wrong. Honor and family meant everything to his brother. There was really only one explanation—the House of Var. King Attor and his cat-shifting nation of savages made for worthy enemies. They were powerful, ruling over the southern half of the small planet. Alek expected the old king to start a war soon. The Var always seemed to be on the brink of it, as if there had not been enough death already. Wars were terrible affairs for their kind, sometimes lasting for fifty to a hundred years with many deaths and seldom any clear progress or victory, just an uneasy truce while each side replenished their warriors and concentrated on rebuilding the population.

It was only by chance that Alek detected the muffled clank of chains on stone. He changed direction, running in shifted form through the forest toward the old rock quarries. The mines had been abandoned centuries ago, but the ruins were still there, overgrown with trees and brush. The sound stopped. Alek paused, listening past his pounding heart. Another clank. The noise was louder than before but still muffled. He crouched to the ground. This was not how Attor usually fought. The Var king was boastful, prideful. But if not Attor or his men, then who? Who would take Bron?

What if there was no enemy? Alek could detect nothing of the cat-shifters. There were no tracks, no scented markings on trees. If Bron had gone for a run in the forest, which was likely by the way the new duchess acted about being married, then it was possible he'd been mad and careless. What if he had fallen down a weakened shaft? Of course, in such a case, the duke should have been able to claw his way out of it.

Nothing about this seemed right.

The clank sounded again. Alek moved toward a sink hole in the ground. He pushed a pile of brush aside. "Bron?"

Nothing.

"Bron, are you down there? Bron?"

It took a moment, but he heard a muffled answer, "Alek? Is that you?"

"Bron, hold on, I'm coming!" He glanced around the forest before dropping himself down into the hole. Light streamed in from above into the dark tunnel. The walls were crumbling stone and the hole smelled of earth and insects. He heard the ticking of tiny creatures behind the stones as the insects crawled around him unseen.

"Have the Var captured you as well? Are you harmed?" Bron asked.

Alek moved toward a boulder and began to push. There were fresh markings on the floor where the stone stood. Someone had recently shoved it into place. The stone scraped. Alek pounded his fists alongside it to knock the boulder loose. It had been jammed against the uneven wall to block a thick metal door. He kicked at the rusted metal to jar it free on its stiff hinges before bracing his feet on the wall to pry it open. Finally, he was able to fit his hand through the opening along the metal edge. He bit back a growl as he broke in to where his brother was held chained to a wall. The hollowed-out prison was pitch black. Bron had been buried alive and left to starve.

Who would do such a thing?

Alek coughed lightly as he breathed in the dust stirred by the old door. "I saw no Var, but that does not mean they are not close. There were boulders against your door. Someone did not want you found."

"Help me with the chains," Bron commanded. They both pulled, using their shifted strength to force the chains free from the wall. The metal pins gave with a loud crack of stone. Bron threw the chains over his shoulder as the cuffs were still attached to his wrists. "How did you find me?"

"Your wife." Alek slid through the broken door frame and passed the dislodged boulder. The old shafts were hardly safe and this one had no support beams, only crumbling stones to form a dilapidated wall.

"Aeron?" Bron asked. "Is she all right?"

"I caught her trying to travel down to the palace with your ceffyl." Alek paused, breathing deeply to sense their surroundings. Tension tightened every muscle. Still, he detected no one. Absentmindedly, he reassured his brother, "She is safe."

Bron nodded. He looked like he wanted to ask more but refrained. Right now they needed to get clear of the old mines and figure out what was happening. Alek didn't volunteer more information about Aeron. Nothing he had to say would be useful. He knew little of the woman but that the gods had chosen her for his brother. In that he had faith she was a good fit to the family honor and a deserving woman. Still, there had been something about the way she denied her marriage to Bron that did not inspire sympathy within him. She had not known Alek and Bron were brothers when she said it. It was dishonorable to deny a marriage, and so soon after the ceremony was finished, especially out of the circle of family.

Alek led the way toward the light. Bron blinked heavily before letting his eyes shift from dragon to human. The human eyes would be less sensitive to the sudden change in brightness.

"Careful," Bron warned. "They disguise their scent. I did not smell them coming for me. I was running and then I was in that dungeon, as if only a second had passed in between."

Alek leapt up the hole. His tone hard as they clawed their way up a narrow shaft toward the light, he asked, "How could you not detect their foulness? Has your bride tainted your thinking so much?"

They appeared on the forest floor. The smell of the mountain instantly replaced the stagnant earth. The forest was still, but for the gentle call of the birds. Bron didn't answer.

Alek continued, "How did the Var know of this

place? We have been all over these mountains and I have never heard of an underground prison. It looks to be a relic of the ancient wars. They must not have expected anyone to find you. I think they left you to rot." Alek gave Bron a meaningful look. "I am glad the gods had other plans for you."

"I owe you much, brother," Bron said, by way of a thank you.

Alek nodded once. "It was your bride who alerted me. I may have been harsh with her." The words were possibly an understatement, but it was all the apology he would make on the matter.

"I will take care of it," Bron said. "I will make her understand."

Alek took a deep breath, ready to sprint. "Can you run? I left our brides at the cabin when I came to track you."

Bron answered by leading the way at full speed. The thick chains bounced against his shifted flesh. Alek followed behind him, keeping pace. With each passing second, he thought more of Kendall. He wanted to get back to her, to know she was all right. The fear was irrational. He would have sensed danger before he left them. The cabin was safe.

Still, a nagging fear in light of the fact that Bron had been captured would not leave him. As they neared the cabin, Bron slowed his pace. Alek breathed deeply and focused his senses. The forest was clear. He detected movement inside the cabin. It was light and nonthreatening.

"Seven out of eight of us found brides," Bron said, pulling his brother's attention away from the women.

Alek frowned at the statement. "All but Mirek, yes. Did they strike you on the head? I know who found brides. Do you not remember that I was at the ceremony?"

Bron matched his brother's look. "My head is fine. My point is that seven of us found brides. Marriage means children and our heirs will grow to power."

"If you try to speak to me of how children are made, I have to tell you, brother, I am not as innocent as you assume." Alek couldn't help his smirk.

"I feel sorry for your bride," Bron returned. "You will probably come at her like a ceffyl male in heat. Do try to remember ladies don't like to be bucked in the head before the mating ritual."

Falling instantly back into the more serious conversation, Alek said, "You think that someone kidnapped you and locked you away in order to stop the next generation of leaders?" Scary as the prospect was, Alek had to admit that it was a good plan. The best way to stop an age-old battle was to ensure the enemy had no future generations to lead or to fight. "If that is true, none of us are safe. We should inform the king and warn the princes."

"And Vladan," Bron added. "I have no desire to start a war with the Var, but who else would do this? Mirek has said nothing about threats from off world."

"It is unlike King Attor to capture a prisoner of high worth only to ignore him. He would want everyone to know about it."

"Perhaps he needed it kept secret." Bron took a step toward the cabin. "And perhaps there was not enough time for his boasting."

Alek hated the Var. The smelly cats were deceitful, prideful and represented nothing but death and war in his mind. His father had felt the same way. It was why the man had preferred to run the mines rather than be on the battlefront. When called, Alek's father had gone to war as was his duty, but he preferred the easy life in the mountains.

"Even if Attor wished to keep it secret, he would have wanted you to know who captured you and abandoned you in the ancient dungeon." Alek paused next to the cabin, out of sight from the windows. He could hear the women moving inside and knew they were safe.

"I'm not sure how much you know about mining," Kendall said, the sound of her beautiful voice muffled by the walls, "but this planet is one of the only mineral-rich sources of the *galaxa-promethium*, a semi-radioactive element that not only has stable isotopes, but whose elements can be harnessed to fuel long voyaging starships. Normally, only very trivial amounts of the element can be found naturally."

Alek forced his attention away from his bride. She was well. There was time to discuss this with his brother before they went inside. "He would have marked the wall, or clawed your skin."

"Who else would dare?" Bron asked.

"Who else would gain by it?" Alek returned. "Perhaps you should speak to your bride."

Bron stiffened and clenched his fist. Alek refused to elaborate on his comment, but he didn't need to. Any further words would have just been insulting. However, it needed to be said. If Aeron's past lover—or lovers—wanted Bron out of the way, it would make sense. What better way to stake claim to the woman than to make it look like her new husband had run out on his marital duties? He couldn't believe that Aeron was behind the kidnapping directly. The gods would not have allowed such a match.

Alek was surprised when Bron didn't hit him. If his brother had even hinted such a thing about Kendall, he would have punched him and rightly so.

"The king told you," Bron stated.

Alek quirked a brow, not understanding. Bron mistook his silence as confirmation.

"It is true. I was unable to resist my bride and consummated the marriage early. This could be nothing more than a punishment from the gods." Bron didn't meet his eyes. "Come. I need a bath. Let us hope this is the end of it."

Alek looked up toward the sky, studying the green tint of the heavens. He couldn't help but wonder if the gods intended to punish him for his own lapse in tradition. He should have resisted Kendall. Yet, how could he have? Just thinking her name caused his body to lurch in reaction. He should have brought her to the bridal procession. He should have waited for her to take off his mask. He should have done many things differently.

"Alek," Bron insisted when he didn't move.

Alek nodded and followed his brother into the cabin.

"It's a certification program. I'm working on finishing Fuelologist and Station Engineer training through the Exploratory Science Commission," Kendall stated. "It made sense, being as I grew up on a space fuel port."

"Who are your people?" Aeron asked.

"They are called Haven, like me, Kendall Haven," Kendall said.

Alek reached out to stop Bron from entering the cabin. He wanted to hear more. He moved too late. His brother pulled the door open, shoving the wood aside much harder than was necessary. It slammed, causing both women to gasp loudly.

"What happened to you?" Aeron demanded, standing within seconds. Relief flooded her face she hurried toward her husband.

Kendall didn't move to greet them. Disappointment filled Alek as he stepped past his brother to move toward the table.

"Spoken like a true wife," he muttered.

Aeron frowned at him. Alek gave her a blank look in return. He wasn't sure why he gave the woman such a hard time, but it most likely had something to do with the way she'd denied her marriage. Perhaps being cold toward Aeron saved him from voicing his frustrations over his own failing marriage.

"It is nothing for you to be concerned over," Bron told his wife.

"Nothing to be concerned over?" Aeron repeated in disbelief. "How can you say that? You disappeared. There was no trace of you anywhere, and then you come back looking like you clawed your way out of a gravesite, and you say it's nothing to be concerned over? Are you daft?"

Alek tried to ignore them as he went toward

Kendall. She didn't run to him, merely watched him approach. What had he expected? That the small time apart would have changed her mind and made her want to be with him forever? Doubtful. If anything, she was probably holding her breath waiting the appropriate amount of seconds before asking him to find her a way off his planet.

"Why?" Bron asked somewhat loudly. "Were you concerned about me?"

"I doubt your wife would dishonor our family name with worry," Alek inserted, reminding them that there were two other people in the cabin. "No woman would want a weak husband who hides behind her skirts."

"Dishonor?" Kendall asked before Aeron could get out whatever sputtering answer was forming on her lips. His new sister-in-law seemed braver now that her husband was by her side. Aeron met Alek's gaze challengingly, nothing like the timid creature he'd first seen coming down alone on the mountain path. Maybe he had misjudged her.

Kendall continued, forcing him to turn his eyes to her. "How is being worried about someone dishonorable?"

Alek wondered at the heat in her question. The answer was so logical it should have been obvious. "You should trust the will of the gods, and in the strength of your man." He lowered his voice so the others wouldn't hear him—unless Bron listened really hard, but the duke's attention was elsewhere. "A man is not a man if he cannot protect what is his, Kendall. Women are soft, fragile. They are to be protected. All men know this."

She arched a brow.

"Why are you looking at me like that?" Alek asked. "What I say is logical."

"So now it's a man thing?" Kendall demanded loudly.

He didn't understand the cause of her irritation, but she was gorgeous with her flushed cheeks and widened eyes. He was overcome with the sudden urge to drag her to one of the back rooms to finish what Aeron had interrupted.

Kendall seemed completely unaware of the fantasies playing in his head. "I'm not sure I like your tone. Are you implying that women are weaker than men? That we should just sit back and let the men folk handle everything?"

"Yes," Alek answered without hesitation.

"Yes?" Kendall repeated. "Did you actually just say that?"

Was she angry with him for speaking the truth? How many ways could he say the same thing? It was logic. Men were stronger. It was a biological fact, at least with every alien race he'd ever heard of. Women were softer, gentler. Even the Draig queen, a natural-born dragon-shifter, was gentler than her husband.

It sounded as if Bron gave a soft laugh. Alek shot a hard glance at his brother.

"Is that what you think? Men are to rule over women?" Bron's wife demanded.

"I would not say rule," Bron answered, his tone much more careful than Alek's had been. "But I do know women should never rule over men—save perhaps the queen over our people, or noblewomen over those beneath her station so long as it is done with benevolence. Between husband and wife there is a clear distinction. Do you not wish for a husband that can protect you and make you proud?"

"There can and should be compromise, but men who are guided too easily by women are not real men," Alek added. What was wrong with these women? "Such a man could not protect you, provide for you, give you strong sons."

"And a woman's role in marriage is what? Cooking and having children?" Kendall demanded. She wrinkled her nose.

"Yes," Alek said. He did not relent. His eyes shifted as the frustration built in him. He would not lie to save her anger.

"I see," Kendall stated. "It's a wonder your gods bothered to give us women brains at all, when really all we need are bellies to hold children and hands to serve our master husbands."

"I did not say—" Alek began.

"Do not say another word," Kendall warned, lifting her hand toward his face. "I have had it with the men in my life trying to tell me what to do. We had an arrangement, if you recall, and I expect you to keep to it."

Behind him, Bron protested to Aeron, "I'd think you would want a strong husband. Why would you wish for a man who cowers behind your skirts and who drops his sword at the first sign of trouble? Such a man is not a man. Such a man would not bring honor to his family. Such a man cannot protect his family."

"Why would we need protection by sword?" Aeron asked.

"Yes, Alek," Kendall stated irately through gritted teeth. "Why would we need protection by sword?"

"The Var," both men stated in unison.

"Our enemy," Bron explained to his wife. Kendall didn't take her eyes from Alek, but he knew she listened to what the high duke was saying. "Many believe there will be another war soon. If there is, we will be expected to lead our men to battle."

"Battle?" Kendall repeated. "If there is a war,

air travel will become dangerous and restricted. I can't be here. I want to go home. I can't get involved with all of this. I need to…" She glanced around the cabin before pushing past him. "I have to get out of here. I can't stay here."

"Kendall!" Alek shouted to stop her as she rushed toward the front door of the cabin. "Kendall, the forest may not be safe. I need you to stay inside while we—*Kendall!*"

7

KENDALL DIDN'T STOP WALKING, even as she heard Alek yelling her name. The fanciful daydream she'd allowed herself to have while talking to Aeron about the Draig men came crashing to a realistic halt. Alek was a barbarian—a stubborn, aggravating barbarian. She'd met his kind before on the fueling dock. They talked all sweet when they wanted something, but eventually their true natures would show themselves in the form of maddening opinions and superior attitudes.

She didn't have time to deal with a barbarian.

"Margot," she whispered. "I have to get to Margot before he loses her as he did me."

She wished she could believe her father would not dare to sell Margot, but the man had no self-control when it came to wagers. She didn't doubt he loved his daughters, but there would be a part of him that would jump at the idea of no longer having familial responsibilities. Kendall took care of everything—the fueling dock, the accounts, Margot. Now that she was gone, her father would spin out of control. As the business started to fail, his quest for that *one big win* would increase and so would the losses.

The thought gave her renewed purpose. She moved in a wide arc around the ceffyl. A short whistle sounded and the beast stood. Startled at the sudden movement, Kendall stumbled to a halt. Alek was at her side within seconds.

"Stop," Alek demanded. "If I am to protect you, you must listen to what I tell you. I won't have you charging angrily about the countryside."

"I may be in your debt, but I am not a slave to be ordered about. You don't own me, Alek." She glared at him.

"Quit saying such things. You—"

She didn't wait to hear what he had to say. "And I wasn't charging. I was—"

"Quit saying such things. You are my wife." He tried to grab her arm.

"Did you just order me to be quiet?"

"You cannot go about calling yourself a slave," he said under his breath. "If others hear you, such a declaration must be publically addressed. I have no wish to see you put yourself into punishment."

"Fine, not a slave but a soldier, whatever you want to call it, but that doesn't change my point. We talked about this. I can't stay here." She pulled away from him. There was something about his stubborn tone that irritated her. She'd noticed it first when he spoke to Aeron, but when he turned that tone on her… Kendall frowned, not liking it one bit. "Which way to your brother Mirek? I understand you needed to detour for your lost brother, but you found Bron. Now I must insist we find Mirek."

"I must insist you come back inside. We detected no Var in the forest, but we don't know what they have planned. We need to take caution. They shouldn't have been able to overtake Bron, especially not in these mountains. Until we know what is happening, you shouldn't be outside alone." His Qurilixian accent rolled softly over her as he lightened his tone. This was more like the Alek who had wooed her in the bridal tent. She was not so easily persuaded by his voice this time, no matter how appealing it sounded.

"Do you really think a war is coming?" She followed him back to the house but kept her distance from him and the standing ceffyl.

"Yes, but not today."

Kendall stopped. "What happened to your brother? His clothes look like he was rolling on the ground and..." She lifted her hand to brush dirt off Alek's shoulder. "...you are dusty."

"I found him underground. He'd been chained to stone and left to starve. Had I not found him, he would have died like that. The gods clearly sent Aeron to us so that I would find Bron and rescue him from death."

That brought her up short and she jerked her hand from him. For a moment, she expected him to laugh in dark humor, but his eyes studied her seriously. "You mean... Is that kind of occurrence normal?"

"No. We are in the mountain territory, very far north of the borderlands. Normally the Var stay on their side. If you must know, it is very unlike them to take an enemy without facing them. I have never heard of the Var attacking us in such a way before, but perhaps it is a new method of warfare they are trying. Now that we are married, they may be coming after us to ensure we do not have children. Or..." He paused, glancing away.

"Or?" Was there a worse explanation than their lives being in danger because they had participated in the marriage ceremony? The Galaxy Brides' uploads had said nothing about signing on for a death sentence or a possible war. They had called the planetary disputes *territorial skirmishes*. To Kendall a territorial skirmish meant fighting over where to make the borders on a map, or who had legal right to certain parts of a fuel mine—the person who owned the mine and had mining permission from the local government, or the person who's land it was under.

"Or the gods are punishing us because we failed to settle our marriages during the ceremony. We broke tradition."

His explanation didn't make her feel better. She hated to tell him that as a kid her roaming fueling dock home had been stationed all over the skies and she'd never seen evidence of his gods. She was sure there was something more beyond the known, but no actual gods who meddled in the lives of their subjects. There were too many aliens with too many varying faiths, and each thought they were right.

"So the Var wish to attack the new marriages?" Kendall said. "I assume this has to do with the mines? Can't you just profit share with them or something?"

"Our disagreements have nothing to do with mining rights. They have their own operations. The bad blood between us goes much deeper."

Kendall concluded their wars must be over a theological matter, which was much worse than monetary reasons. "Then my leaving will solve both our problems. You will live and I will be able to take care of what I need to."

"That is not what I was saying," Alek protested.

"But it is what you said," she countered. "I am in danger if I stay here."

"No, it is not customary to hurt women, even in times of war. They are too rare on this planet. You —" His voice came to an abrupt stop and he held up his hand.

Panicked by the look on his face, she quickly took in their surroundings. She heard nothing, saw nothing. Kendall automatically slipped between him and the cabin, fearful of what would make this strong guy go on high alert. "What is it?"

"Quiet," he ordered.

She leaned into his side, next to the protective strength of his body while still being able to see past him to the valley.

"Have you heard of the Tyoe?" Alek suddenly asked.

"Tyoe?" She stiffened and looked up at him. His face was so close she could see the texture of his skin. The tiniest of scars ran along his jaw. She hadn't noticed it before, it was so small. She breathed deeply, taking in his raw masculine scent.

"They are a race of aliens."

Kendall shook her head, confused by the

sudden change in conversation. "I haven't met one, but I know who the Tyoe are by reputation. They run fuel mines all over the universe. They're profiteers."

"Would these profiteers attack us to set up a mining colony?"

"I…" She shrugged. "I don't know. Why would they? I'm guessing they'd just try to buy the mining rights, or at the very least trade for them. I doubt any corporation or business entity would attack without first trying to acquire the mines in another legal way. What makes you think the Tyoe are attacking?"

Alek nodded to the cabin door. His eyes shifted with gold. "They are talking of it inside. Aeron worked as a contracted civilian analyst for the Federation Military and came to us to warn of a Tyoe attack."

"I thought this planet was not a part of the Federation Alliance." If they were, it would have been easier to get a flight off world. Knowing there was no immediate danger in the forest, she relaxed but didn't back away. News of an aerial attack by a technologically advanced, profiteering race was hardly a comfort. Suddenly, swords and dungeons weren't sounding too bad.

"We are not." He leaned closer to the door and in the process closer to her. "Aeron says the Federation has little interest in our planet or our people, but for our mining operations. They think us primitive with no military or scientific value other than the ore. As long as we mine the ore, they have seen no reason to interfere with our process."

Kendall frowned. They shouldn't be listening to the other couple's private conversation. Yet she wasn't really listening. She couldn't hear anything beyond the door. "The Tyoe have mining bases all over the galaxy and are really good at what they do. I know this from some classes I took that covered mining processes and galaxy law."

"And they would make war to establish a new base?"

"I honestly cannot tell you, Alek. Is the Federation offering to help? It might be wise to accept. They have many resources. A lot of planets do well under Federation Alliance. You would be protected. You—"

"No. The Federation does not care as long as they get the ore, and we have no wish to be a part of the Federation's alliance." He glanced down at her. "Is this why you want to leave? You also think us primitive and unable to defend ourselves against alien threats?"

Alek's shifted eyes captured hers and she couldn't look away. She shook her head in denial.

Her voice lowered by small degrees. "No. I find you very capable."

Where did that comment come from? Was she flirting with him? Now? Seconds ago she'd been so angry and scared she wanted to throw him off the cliff if he stood in her way. Her attraction to him changed nothing. He was still a barbarian. He was still stubborn. She was still leaving.

Kendall let her lids fall over her eyes. She felt the full force of her situation trying to crumble over her. It loomed overhead like a comet frozen in time, waiting for the perfect moment to crash. The only thing between her and her world falling completely apart in a steaming explosion of rock and heartache was Alek. She felt safe with him. He might have primitive ideas about who and what men and women were, but he had saved her from her repossession. He had made it possible for her to get away from those who would force her to marry a stranger.

The reality she *was* married hadn't fully hit her until that second as she stared into his eyes. Married. How could she have agreed to something that was such a big deal? She'd been so focused on getting back to Margot that she hadn't stopped to think it through, not really. Marriage. Married. She was this man's wife. Even if it was a marriage of convenience, it was still a marriage, and that kind of commitment meant something to her.

"Alek," she whispered. Kendall tried to take a step back but she was stopped by the cabin's exterior wall. The air was cool, but not cold. It caressed her face as it slipped between them. "Alek, I—"

He stopped her words with a kiss. The warmth of his tongue instantly slid into her mouth.

Alek, I'm sorry. I should never have married you. It was wrong. It was selfish. It was…

The words never left her. Everything she needed to say to him died in that kiss. She tried to hold on to her logic. It was no use. She felt the unfulfilled desire rise up within her. It had shimmered beneath the surface since their shared kisses on the trail on the way to the cabin. She glided her fingers up his arms to cup his face. He swept his tongue back and forth across her mouth, teasing and exploring at the same time. They had been alone in the tent, in the dark, and yet this moment felt more intimate than those midnight touches.

If lips could search and plead, his were doing just that. For the longest time, he simply kissed her, holding her trapped against the side of the house. Slowly, his body came up against hers, brushing softly before pressing firmly. His hips rotated toward her, moving along her stomach. He slid his hands down the side of the house to grab hold of her ass. With a measured show of strength, he lifted her off the ground. She moved her hands from his face to his neck. She held on. Her thighs parted naturally to accept him.

Their legs tangled in the long length of her skirt. She fell back against the house, propped up by his hands. His lips followed her briefly before pulling back. The bulky material between them made it difficult to wrap her legs around his waist. Yellow intensity swirled in his gaze, molten hot like liquid gold. She felt the fire in him, the passion, and it was all directed at her. The intensity of that moment both frightened and exhilarated her. She tried to speak, but her brain couldn't form a coherent word and all that came out was a soft, breathy moan.

"Come," he said, more of a command than request. Her legs dropped a little too quickly and she was glad the house was there to keep her from falling.

"Where?" she whispered, her body weak like the cloth doll she had as a child. He took her wrist and pulled her around the side of the house. When they reached a small enclosed area, part wall, part trees and brush, he drew her against him once more.

"Is this safe?"

"Yes." He kissed her softly. "Do you hear the birds?"

She nodded.

"They change their song when the Var are in the forest. There is something about the scent of a cat-shifter that sets them off. I will know if we are not safe." He tried to kiss her again, but she pulled her face away.

"Bron didn't know. He was captured. Wouldn't he have heard the birds?"

Alek's expression fell. He looked as if she had slapped him. "You are justified in questioning my family's honor in light of what happened to Bron. He should not have been captured as he was. We have been fighting the Var our whole lives. There is no explanation as to how he was overtaken by them unless the gods intervened. To be fair to my brother, not everyone can detect the more subtle differences in the birds' songs. I have a special gift when it comes to understanding animals. I've had it since I was born. It is why I am the Top Breeder of the ceffyls."

"I did not mean to insult your family. I am sure your brother is a fine fighter. Perhaps he didn't see the Var because it is the Tyoe who took him." Her sanity started to come back as his kisses dried from her lips. Desire and fear warred inside her. "The Tyoe are advanced." Before he could comment on her choice of words, she quickly amended, "That is to say, they have technological advancements you do not employ on this planet."

"We have not had any conflict with the Tyoe, so it would seem unlikely. We have dealt with the Var since before anyone can remember. I do not have answers, but I will not stop until I find them." He touched her face. "I will protect you with my life, Kendall. You have my word."

"I am not foolish enough to dismiss such a gesture. While I remain here, I will gladly accept your offer of protection. I am not equipped for planetary survival. I've only read about it." She leaned unconsciously closer to him. "But I hope protection does not become necessary."

"Planetary life is not so bad." He cupped her face and gave her the smallest of smiles. Lids fell heavily over his liquid gaze. The gold color captured her attention, drawing her in to him. The side of the house felt intimate, secure, even as they were outside surrounded by trees. "There is something to be said for having a home that does not move."

"Technically planets move. We're moving right now."

He closed his eyes and chuckled.

"I think I can feel the ground shifting. I feel a

little lightheaded." She slid her hands onto his arms. "I think I need to hold on to something."

His eyes didn't open as he leaned his face closer. She felt the heat of his body, the tickle of his breath against her lips. He waited for her mouth to touch his, letting his lips hover just beyond final contact. How could she resist?

This time when they kissed she knew there would be no stopping their consummation. The rush of denied desire built once more, untamed and raw. She pressed her mouth to his, moaning into an instantly deep kiss. Their lips ground passionately against each other, almost painful, yet somehow still pleasurable in their desperation.

The hard, cool stone of the house kept her upright as his body molded into hers. Every sensation magnified itself until her nerves stung and her thoughts swam in her head. The full length of her body tingled. Her arms restlessly moved as she tried to touch him everywhere at once. She tugged at his shirt. The smell of dust stirred around them and she gave a soft moan.

His kiss lightened, becoming gentler, as if the sound of her voice made him aware of how delicate she was. Kendall didn't feel delicate. She felt needy and confident. She wanted to rip off his clothes, throw him to the ground and forget everything else. The mindless temptation was too much to fight. Reason left her until the only reality was the man before her.

Alek slid his hand along the back of her thigh and hitched up her leg. She pulled at his clothes. The warmth of his hard flesh met her fingers as she explored his chest beneath the tunic shirt. He flicked his tongue over her mouth. Their bodies became a frenzy of movements. His hands seemed to be everywhere at once.

Before Kendall could think, she found herself stripped of her clothing with loud rips and tears of material, and his naked body against hers. Pleasure, hot and sure, flowed over her. The attraction she felt for him seemed destined to be.

Kendall pulled her mouth from his, breathing hard. Destined to be? Did she suddenly believe in twentieth-century Earth stories of true love and destiny? Fated mates? True love? Soul joining?

The answer *yes* tried to whisper its way through her brain. She knew better. Deep down, logic knew better. This was lust, not love. This was passion and pleasure, not a matter of the heart. There was no such thing as one true love. How could there be? With all the people in the known universes, and those they hadn't even made contact with, how could there be only one person meant for another? Alek and his people seemed to believe it. Maybe that was why she was thinking such nonsense. Or perhaps it was the way he was kissing her neck, licking and biting and moaning as he did so.

All the teasing of flesh accumulated into a jolt of excitement as he drew his body to hers. He lifted her off the ground, holding her against the wall as he opened her legs. The press of his shaft along her sex sent chills over her skin. He did not lift his face from her neck as he thrust forward. Like a well-trained marksman, he hit his target without first testing the depths. She stiffened as he filled her, stretching her muscles to fit his larger size. A low, animalistic growl escaped him and he barely gave her time to adjust before he began to move. He thrust, in and out, working his body against hers. His hips found a steady rhythm, taking and giving at the same time. Each grind of their bodies bespoke of hunger and need.

Alek rode her hard. He kept her pinned to the unforgiving wall. She could but take what he gave her.

It was over too quickly. Kendall didn't want the moment to end and yet, as her orgasm hit her like a rogue fuel cell igniting, she had no choice but let it explode. She tensed, trembling and stiff at the same time. As her body clamped onto him, his low grunt resounded against her moist neck. He jerked his release into her, keeping his body deep inside hers.

A long, hot, sticky moment passed before he let

her go. Her feet slid to the ground and leaves crushed beneath her shoes. Logic tried to invade her thoughts, but she didn't want to think. Unbidden, she yawned. The relaxation of her climax triggered sleepiness.

"Come," Alek said softly, urging her to follow him toward the front of the house. "It is quiet inside and you should rest."

Kendall merely nodded.

KENDALL STARED AT THE WALL, so exhausted she could barely move. Alek had left her alone so that he might bathe. He'd insisted she rest after being awake for so long, and that she could bathe when she awoke.

A small trail of light entered through the bottom of the bedroom door. It felt strange to be sleeping on a planet, with light, so much light. Space was dark for the most part, and her body was used to a strict schedule dictated by timed lights located high on the wall inside each metal room. Green was morning. Yellow meant afternoon. Red meant it was time to sleep. Here, there was just green-tinted daylight. She realized her body waited for the darkness that wouldn't come, for a red light to signal that her day was done and that it was all right to be tired and to sleep.

The room was big, as was the bed. She huddled near the edge, wrapped in thick blankets to make her world feel smaller. There were no temperature controls, so even though it wasn't too hot or too cold, it wasn't exactly right. Then there was the noise. It was faint and rare, but it was there if she listened hard enough. Every once in a while some wild creature outside would yell or screech outside. So she stared at the wall, watching it, her mind unable to shut off as she imagined how thin and fragile the building stone was compared to the rein-forced metal of a ship's haul.

When she'd been with Alek outside, in a frenzy of passion and lust, she had felt something. It wasn't a feeling she wanted to analyze too closely. She was an educated, logical, practical woman. In extreme situations bonds could form between people. She was on a new world, stressed, worried about Margot, desperate to save her sister, and Alek was the only person to show her kindness since her repossession.

There was something else bothering her too. They'd called her abduction a *repossession*, not a seizure of property. One could only repossess some-thing they had possessed to begin with. She'd been too stressed by her situation to think about it before, but a repossession order only could mean this wasn't the first time her father had gambled and lost her to the casino. Only, the other times, he must have won—or bought—her back before she found out about it. Somehow, the knowledge made her feel all the more alone in the world. How could the man have risked her like that? He knew the kinds of things that happened to enslaved women in the universe. She was lucky she had been sold to a legitimate marriage broker. She could have easily ended up in a Kintok sex-slave ring and forced to spend the rest of her life on a pleasure ship, indulging their clientele's fetish games before ultimately being launched into deep space like trash when she became too used up to earn a profit.

When the stress of her thoughts had eaten a hole through her stomach and chest, she was forced to close her eyes. She couldn't move even if she'd wanted to. The only thing that awaited her on the other side of sleep was the nightmares that could have very well been a reality.

8

ALEK LET KENDALL SLEEP. The poor woman looked completely worn. She didn't move when he crawled into bed next to her for a few hours, or when he crawled back out. It was no wonder. She'd been awake for nearly two days. The nights were a bit brighter up here, so it was possible she hadn't even noticed the hours that passed. Alek was used to working for days at a time and hadn't thought much about it. He should have been more conscientious of his new bride.

They had gotten a late start when they'd traveled up the mountain. Then his leaving to save Bron, the fight, making love, the aftermath of making love… It all added up to some very long hours. Alek smiled. At least it had ended well. Very well.

He stood alone next to the front door watching the distant skies. The forest sounded normal. There were no Var roaming the woods this morning. Everything in his gut told him that the Var were not responsible for Bron's abduction. Could it be the gods had punished them for their botched ceremonies? Would he be next? Plucked off the ground and buried somewhere as punishment? Or was there a less mystical reason?

The Tyoe.

Alek frowned. He knew nothing of the Tyoe race. Such things they left to Mirek to deal with.

Alek loved his home world, so it wasn't hard for him to imagine another race of aliens wanting to take it for themselves. The location of Qurilixen in the star system made it isolated with very low space travel. People generally didn't come to the planet unless they had a reason to. The Federation left them alone. The carefully cultivated decision to appear low-tech—while aesthetically pleasing—had the added benefit of hiding their true defensive power to the rest of the universes. It was the same reason they didn't let it be known they were shifters. In the old days, some liked to capture his kind and force them into militaries. He remembered sitting around campfires as a young boy, listening to his elders debate the idea of hiring outside corporations to bring brides to the planet. In the end, it had been decided their need for women outweighed the risk of lost privacy. No women equaled no future generations to protect the privacy of. Not all generations would be so lucky as to have a ship filled with single women crash in the forest, as had happened once in the past. Those who were against the Galaxy Brides contract cited the incident, saying the gods had provided for them. Not everyone was willing to take that chance. In the end, the compromise had been to carefully dictate the terms of any information distributed about their kind. Galaxy Brides didn't care, so long as they got their annual shipment of ore to fuel all their ships.

"I thought I sensed you awake," Bron said from the door. Alek had heard him moving around inside the house.

"I am considering the Tyoe," Alek answered.

"Then you heard what my wife said?"

Alek nodded.

"That will save me having to explain it. That's why I came out to talk to you." Bron took his place next to his brother, leaning against the wall and looking at the sky. "I thought you might have heard what she said. However, I did question her more about it. Aeron came here to try to protect us. I have no reason to doubt her concerns."

"Concerns or fear?" Alek asked with a deep

frown. Aeron clearly had no faith in her husband's protective abilities. Then again, who was he to speak on the subject? His bride mentioned leaving him in almost every conversation they had.

"I will hit you, brother," Bron warned.

Alek nodded and said nothing. Apologizing wasn't exactly a Draig trait. He had no practice at it.

"She told me that fear was merely a chemical reaction in the body and that it could not be controlled." Bron sighed. "Perhaps it is some kind of trait from her line of humanoid."

Alek chuckled. "I'm glad it is you with the emotional bride then. If that's true, it will be fun watching you try to calm her when she gets worked up into some female state. Physical, I can well handle as a man and a warrior. I will leave you to the speaking of feelings. Clearly the gods thought you better suited to such a task."

"Go ahead and laugh," Bron said. "I heard Kendall got sick off the smell of cooking meat. You'll be lucky to get a food-simulated meal out of her. At least my bride can cook."

"Mine looks good naked," Alek countered. He liked the easy conversation as it lightened their more serious moods.

"As does mine." Bron's tone dropped. "Mm, as does mine."

"Before I lose you to your marriage bed, what is it you are trying to tell me?" Alek pushed up from the wall. He really wanted to run, but he couldn't leave Kendall unattended. That was how Bron had been captured.

Bron's smile faded. "Aeron has concerns about Kendall. The women had time alone while we were otherwise engaged. She also knows your wife from the ship. I feel honor bound to tell you."

Alek tensed. Every muscle in his body on alert.

"She said when they spoke, Kendall sounded secretive and strange, like she was hiding something."

Alek stared at the ground. His voice hard, he asked, "What exactly did your wife say?"

"That Kendall is unsure of staying here as a bride. That she was being secretive, and though Aeron is not one to begrudge a woman her secrets, she is not convinced I should tell you about the Tyoe until you are sure of Kendall's reasons for coming to this planet." Bron paused, moving tentatively closer. "Are you listening?"

"I heard every word. Continue."

"Her reasoning is sound, in a way," Bron continued. "The odds that more than a couple of women came here on the Galaxy Brides ship for reasons other than marriage seem highly unlikely.

Aeron came to warn us. The gods saw fit to have her stay with me."

"And the gods did not send me Kendall?" Alek still didn't trust himself to move. He thought of the forest the night of their weddings. He'd been so close to crushing the crystal and accepting loneliness. Did the gods send him Kendall for another reason? Not as a bride, but for him to watch? He didn't want to believe it, but nothing about his bridal ceremony made sense. What did he really know about her? He knew men had put a tracking device on her and seemed determined not to let her go unless she had a caretaker. Did those men track her even now?

"I am too old to start questioning the will of the gods. They sent Kendall to you just as they sent Aeron here to warn us and marry me. Our fate is in the hands of the gods." Bron lifted his chin. "The rest of the galaxy might not see our technology, but it does not mean we are a backward people who cannot defend ourselves against an enemy. Let the Tyoe come. We will be ready."

Alek ignored his brother's proud testament to their people and redirected the conversation back to his bride. "Is that all you have to say about Kendall?"

"No." Bron did not move closer. Alek could tell his brother did not want to speak his mind but rather felt he had to. "I find it suspect she appeared at such a time, as the Tyoe have started their attacks. We both heard what Kendall said. She is trying to finish her Fuelologist and Station Engineer training through the Exploratory Science Commission. She probably knows more about the ore than even Vlad does. She could be here to test samples for the ESC. She also said she was raised on a space fuel port. It is possible she has dealt with the Tyoe or was approached by them. If they are such a powerful force in the fuel mining trade, they would be in a very good position to offer something valuable to her in return, be it a job or money or recommendations. What if they sent her here to spy on our mines? To discover how we operate? To find our weaknesses?"

Bron's words were an insult and Alek responded the only way he could. He threw a punch. Bron expected the blow and shifted at the last second. Alek's fist landed hard against his brother's armored jaw, sending Bron sprawling to the ground.

"My wife is not a spy," Alek said in warning. What else could he do? Admit that he didn't really know, that his wedding ceremony hadn't gone according to tradition?

Bron growled up at his brother before letting

his features mold back to human flesh. "Better now?"

Alek nodded and reached down to help the man up. "What do you propose? I can take Kendall to the palace to warn the king." He didn't want to take her to Mirek, not yet. Any excuse to avoid giving her a way off planet was one he was willing to take. "You can take your bride to Mirek to see what he knows about the Tyoe. I admit I do not read all of his ambassador reports. It is possible he has dealt with these aliens before and will know if they are what we are dealing with now."

Bron gave a short laugh as he dusted off his pants. "I don't read the reports either, but don't tell him. I think Mirek enjoys writing them."

"I once told him I found his diplomatic missions fascinating and asked for more details in future accountings," Alek admitted.

Bron laughed harder. "Is that why they doubled in size?"

Alek's laughter joined his brother's as he nodded emphatically. "I thought about sending him a report on the breeding production of the ceffyls and then quizzing him about it in conversation, but I was afraid he'd like it and I'd be stuck doing them for the rest of my life."

"Mirek does like his paperwork. We will gladly leave him to it, and to the off world ambassadorial duties." Bron took a calming breath. "I will take Aeron to the palace this morning. She has already been told. After I report to the king, and assure him that my marriage is settled—"

"Is it?" Alek interrupted, instantly jealous and hating that he felt the emotion.

"More or less," Bron answered elusively. "Anyway, after I tell our uncle my marriage is settled and about the attacks, I will check in with palace security and see if they have heard anything from space."

Alek nodded. Hidden near the royal palace, disguised as a mountain peak, the Draig kept a highly advanced communications and watch tower. The security team monitored the stars at all times. "Then you want me to go to Mirek?"

"No. After I tell the king I will go to Mirek to talk to him about the mines and the Tyoe."

"Then what would you have me do?" Alek frowned. "We can cover more territory if we both go."

"As the duke, I am ordering you to stay with your bride. Settle your marriage. Find out why she has come to our world. Hit me all you want, but we need to know if she is a spy sent to help overthrow us. Also, the communication lines between the mountain settlements and the palace have been neglected for far too long. It is time we repaired them. You can start with our cabin. It will give you a task while you are here."

"You are exercising your authority of title over me?" Alek asked, shocked by the very notion. His bother hadn't used his rank on him since they were kids. Even then it hadn't gone over too well.

"Yes. This is too serious of a threat, and I will act accordingly." Bron softened his tone. "I also need you to watch the forest for signs of an enemy. You know these woods better than most. You can sense the animals in a way many can't. Since this is where I was when I was taken, this is where you should remain to investigate."

Everything he said made sense, but Alek didn't have to like it. However, the one very positive part of being ordered to stay was that he couldn't take Kendall to see Mirek. He was duty bound to stay at the cabin, alone, with her. He suddenly smiled.

Bron took a step back. "That was not the reaction I was expecting."

"One moment. You said the communication lines?" Alek grimaced. "You want *me* to repair them?" He barely recalled studying the schematics as a kid. The system was old and had been neglected for decades.

"I was hoping that part of the order wouldn't sink in until after I left." Bron grinned. "Better you than me. I don't remember where we kept the circuit box."

Alek scratched his head. Come to think of it, he didn't remember either. He was about to answer when Bron slammed his fist into the side of his face, hitting human flesh. Alek stumbled back, instantly tense and ready to spar.

Bron was halfway in the door. "I owed you that from yesterday when you commented on my bride. Speak of her like that again and it will be much worse. Now we are even."

"Cursed dragon," Alek swore, mumbling as he rubbed his sore jaw. His blood pumped quickly through his veins and he could have easily followed the high duke inside to finish the fight, but he refrained only because Kendall still slept. Besides, he was inclined to forgive his brother. After all, Bron's orders just bought him more time to convince his bride that she was meant to be his…forever.

9

"WHAT DO you mean we can't leave?" Kendall stared at Alek in disbelief. Her brain was still foggy from oversleeping and she was sure she hadn't heard him correctly.

"My brother has gone to the palace to speak to the king. He ordered me to stay here for the time being. I am not backing out of what I promised you, but I cannot leave the cabin by noble order." Alek's voice sounded strange as he busied himself with some absurd business of pushing against different parts of the smooth wall.

"Then give me the ceffyl beast and point me in the right direction," Kendall demanded. Fear for Margot weighed heavily on her. She needed to find her sister. "I need to return home. You promised to take me to Mirek."

"Bron and Aeron took both ceffyls. We thought it would be best if they had the extra speed. The most immediate threat must be dealt with first." Alek ran his hands over the wall in long sweeps, still not looking at her. He had changed his clothes to a dark-blue tunic with silver threading along the edges. The tunic was designed like a long shirt that hung to his knees and split at the sides, opening to reveal his thighs. His pants were flowing and loose around his legs.

A little self-conscious about her appearance, Kendall brushed her fingers through her hair. She pulled the strands forward to study the red tips of the blonde, noticing that the color seemed strangely faded. She doubted these men would have access to a beauty droid she could use. Then, determining it didn't matter, she shook herself back to the subject at hand.

"You are a grown man. Surely you can come and go as you please?" Kendall tried to move to the side to better see his face. He glanced at her but didn't stop what he was doing as he turned a corner and began the same bizarre ritual of touching every inch of the wall.

"Had he ordered me as man, yes, that is true. He ordered me as the high duke. I cannot disobey." Alek again glanced in her direction but did not hold her gaze long.

"You…" She pointed at him, anger boiling inside her. "You did this on purpose. You want me to stay here. You had your brother order you to stay in this cabin. You gave him the ceffyls so I would be trapped because you know I can't navigate the mountains alone."

Finally, he stopped and turned to her. "You think I purposefully trapped you here?"

"I think it's pretty obvious," Kendall returned. "I wouldn't last a day on foot out there. I heard the wild animals through the wall last night. That forest is not safe."

"Animals?" He furrowed his brow in confusion. "You mean the ambient sound system? I could have turned it off. I told you to pick your room and that is the one Vlad likes to stay in when he comes to the cabin. He sleeps better with the noise. Once you lie on the bed, it triggers the system. Choose another room if that one displeases you."

The information did make her feel a little better, but it didn't change anything. "I wouldn't last in your wilderness. It would be foolish for me to try, and you know it. You want me to stay. I want to go. You promised to take me."

"I remember what I promised." Alek suddenly raised his voice in exasperation. She jolted in surprise at the harsh sound and automatically backed away from him.

"I said we would leave the ceremony ground for my home. I did not say how long it would take us to arrive there. I did not promise there wouldn't be unforeseen duties along the way that I must attend to. I did not intend for this to happen, but it has. I will speak with Mirek about finding you a safe ride off world just as soon as I am able. I did not promise it would be fast."

"I see. You can't break your word to take me to Mirek to find a ride, but your brother can order you to delay your promise with some bogus command."

"For your information…" He took a deep breath and lowered his voice. The hard note to his words was more frightening than his almost-yelling before. "This is not just about you staying here as my bride. I am ordered here to repair the old communication system so that we may be better prepared should an attack happen. I am ordered here to discover…" He sighed and waved his hand in dismissal. Alek turned back to the wall and renewed his efforts of feeling the surface.

When he didn't continue, she prompted, "Discover what?"

"What I can about who was in the forest and what is happening here," he mumbled.

"If the aliens were here, wouldn't it be safer to be with your brother? The whole safety-innumbers thing?" Kendall sighed in exasperation. "And what are you doing molesting the poor wall like that?"

"I am looking for hidden latches. When I said the old communication system, I meant the ancient communication system. None of us can remember where the panel is hidden, it has been so long—wait, I think I found…" He tapped the wall several times. Nothing happened. The smooth surface didn't appear any different from the rest of the house. Drawing his hand back, he slammed his fist down hard. A small panel slid open. Little particles of dust stirred around him as he peered inside. "What do we have…?"

Curious, Kendall leaned forward. The compartment smelled musty. Inside, there were two deeply set shelves with rows of glass and metal bottles lined up on top of them. The bulbous shape of one reminded her of her chemical science classes. "What is it? Chemical vials? Potions? Medicines?"

"My great-grandfather's liquor stash," Alek answered, grinning. "We thought he hid it at the castle home. My family has spent years trying to find it, like a treasure hunt." He reached inside and pulled out an ugly red bottle. "This is a very fine bottle of Qurilixian rum. According to family legend, my great-grandfather sneaked into the Var palace and stole several bottles from the liquor storage."

Alek handed her the bottle to look at. Kendall couldn't read the strange markings on the side. When she shook the bottle, the liquid appeared thick. "I think it has gone bad."

Alek took it from her. "Mm, no, it looks perfect."

"It looks like mineral sludge."

"Oh, it would appear the legend about the Var stash was right." Alek put the Qurilixian rum back on the shelf and then pulled out a smaller bottle. He wrinkled his nose in disgust. "Nef."

"What's nef?" Kendall wondered at his distasteful reaction to the stuff.

"The Var favor it to keep their passion in check. King Attor teaches his subjects to go against their wild nature. The Var nobles take many half-mate wives instead of one true mate. Those who cannot afford to barter for several brides have one, but the king discourages affection."

"Half-mate?"

"The concept is hard to explain if you are not a shifter. Think of it as a partial wife, an acquirement, not a mate to the soul." Alek hurried on before she could ask him about his evasive tone. "The Var king has—I'm not sure the exact count— around three hundred wives?"

"On a planet with a small female population?" Kendall asked in surprise. "Is that why you don't have enough women to marry? The Var king took them all?"

"King Attor did marry some local women, but mostly he trades for them with alien visitors to his territory."

Before she could stop herself, she asked, "How can a man satisfy so many women?"

Alek chuckled darkly. "He can't, which is what makes the hoarding of women so abhorrent. Women are nothing but a collection to him. Attor is a greedy man. There is no redeemable quality to him or his practices."

"Why don't they leave?"

"He is king. The wives do not ask us for our interference." Alek set the bottle back down and pushed it away from the others. "If the gods wanted us to take them from the king, the women would make our crystals glow. Until such a time there is no reason for us to steal Attor's brides if they do not wish to be stolen."

"And the nef helps him satisfy more women?" She looked closely at it.

"The nef controls the shifter beast inside us. When a shifter drinks it, their passions are tempered back so they can't lose control when it comes to sex. If other humanoids drink it, ones who are not shifters, then it has the opposite effect. It causes uncontrollable passion."

"So they drug the women to feel uncontrollable passion for them, while at the same time drugging themselves to feel less?" Kendall frowned in disgust. "These Var don't sound very likeable."

"That is putting it mildly. There is a reason we are constantly at war with them. They are dishonorable beasts. If we let them run wild around this planet, chaos would ensue. Shifters are not meant to half-mate to many women." Alek turned his serious expression to her.

She realized how close she'd gotten to him. He smelled clean and fresh. His clothes were laundered and held the faint trace of forest leaves. She took a deep breath before remembering she had yet to bathe. Alek's eyes turned to her mouth as if he would kiss her. She took a quick, self-conscious step away from him, blocking any sexual advance he might try to make.

"Can you show me how to activate the water bath?" she asked.

"Of course. I will find you fresh clothes as well."

Kendall looked down at the long tunic shirt she wore as a dress. It fell nearly to her ankles. He'd given it to her before she slept since he'd torn the wedding gown. She hugged her arms around her waist and nodded. "I would appreciate that. Thank you."

ALEK SLID the secret panel closed and tried not to listen to the sound of Kendall bathing. The excitement he'd felt at solving the old family mystery of the treasure hunt lessened as a wave of sadness washed through him at Kendall's withdrawal. He wished he could read her thoughts, but she forcefully denied his mind's probing. When—*if*—she accepted him and their marriage, they would connect. He would feel inside her and she would feel inside him. Their emotions would join. It was part of the natural mating process. He felt his mind trying to connect to hers, but he came up against an invisible shield. The physical twinge of rejection radiated around his heart, causing it to ache.

The married men told him that when the process was complete, he'd be able to hear his wife in his mind, calling to him when she wanted him. He wanted to ask Kendall to open up to him, to all they could be to each other, but how could he form such words? He would not dishonor himself by getting on his knees and begging her to love him.

Perhaps it was better she couldn't feel inside him. If they connected, if she felt his desperation for her, would she reject him? Would she leave anyway? Her going would be hard enough as it was, but if they connected on the deepest of levels the loss would become all that more potent and raw. Not to mention the shame he felt at such insecurity. Men were supposed to be brave and strong, not filled with doubts.

Was this why the gods had made him wait so long to marry? They knew he wouldn't be worthy. They knew, deep inside, he'd be terrified of losing Kendall.

Alek didn't know how to deal with fear, so he swallowed it down deep inside and determined never to think of it again. If he ignored it, it would go away.

WATER WAS a strange yet wonderful experience. Kendall had felt it on her skin when she'd been on top of Alek during their bath in the tent, but never had she submersed herself fully into the stuff. On a ship, water was one of those closely guarded resources that was usually rationed—especially when gambling fathers lost half the supply gaming.

The more she thought about it, the more she realized just how sad her childhood really had been. She'd spent her whole life chasing after her father, trying to keep the family together, trying to raise Margot, trying to go to school. Here, on this planet, was the first time she had no real responsibilities. Even as she enjoyed the break, it worried her even more. Without her constant monitoring, the fueling dock could have been run completely into the ground. Her father knew how to do the books but wouldn't. Margot had a temper, and if she was mad at Kendall for leaving who knows what the child would do. Between her father's neglect and her own hot-headedness, Margot could already be on her way into a self-destructive spiral.

The knot in her chest instantly came back. The feeling of helplessness was worse than the stress of responsibility. The not knowing ate away at her insides until she wanted to vomit the bile churning inside her stomach. She had to find a way home. A tear slipped over her cheek, then another.

She drew her knees up so they poked out of the warm water and leaned her head onto them. "Please, someone help me, I need to get home. Just help me get home."

ALEK GRABBED his chest and made a quick dash for the front door. Once outside, he took a deep breath and then another. Despite his better judgment, he'd been trying to sense a hint of what Kendall was feeling. The tiny glimpse of pain inside her was so overwhelming to his senses that he'd had to block her in order to catch his breath. Out of all the things he'd expected to find in her—fear, longing, budding love she tried to deny—that kind of pain had not been on the list.

"Please, someone help me, I need to get home. Just help me get home," she'd whispered. He was so focused on her that he'd heard her clearly, even though the words were not meant for him.

How could he expect her to stay if she wanted to go that badly? Logic told him to guard his heart, but his upbringing told him to trust the gods. In the end, none of it mattered. He loved his wife. He'd known it from that first moment. He didn't need the crystal to tell him, or the gods to show him. He loved his wife and that was why letting her go would probably kill him.

For the first time in his life, he thought maybe the Var were on to something with their nef. Maybe numbing the feelings inside of him was the answer—the only answer he had. He stood frozen, staring at the countryside but not seeing it. Only when he heard Kendall get out of the bath did he move. Turning, he went back inside. Each step was forced as he went to meet her as she came out into the hall.

"We will leave here in a few hours to go to Mirek. I will find you a ride home." Alek couldn't meet her gaze. "I put clean clothes on the bed, two doors down on the left. I'm sorry they were cut for a man, but they should suffice until we reach my castle home to arrange for transportation."

"But…?"

It took everything in him to stand before her. He heard a droplet of water fall from her hair to the floor. Through his peripheral vision he saw the drying linen clinging to her damp body. The thin barrier fueled a desire that did not need fueling.

"What about your brother's order?" she asked.

"I don't have what I need to fix the communication network, and whatever creature was in the forest is no longer here. I promised to help you and that is what I'm going to do." He could barely breathe. His hands shook and he had to concentrate to keep from reaching out and grabbing her. He pressed his lips tightly together, resisting the urge to beg her to stay.

"I don't know what to…" She touched his arm. He stiffened. "Thank you, Alek. For everything. Thank you. I will find a way to repay you, I promise."

"There is no debt between us." He pulled his arm away. Her touch shot fire through him. When he looked at her face, he noticed tiny stress lines had lifted somewhat from her expression. He refused to feel inside her again. The relief he imagined to be there would surely be worse than the pain.

KENDALL WATCHED as Alek walked stiffly away from her to go outside. He didn't look at her, didn't smile. She'd been almost too stunned to speak when he made the blunt announcement. However, the immense relief she imagined such a thing would bring did not come. Instead, she felt an overwhelming sadness.

There was nothing to be done about it. She had a life and she needed to get back to it. Once she was on the fueling dock things were going to change. Her father better be prepared, because Kendall was going to be taking over. Hollow or not, that was her future.

In the bed chamber he indicated, she found a neatly folded stack of clothes next to a plate of food on a small table. The cold meats and vegetables were sandwiched between slices of blue bread. She hesitated before biting into it. The flavor was different than the food she was used to getting from the simulator, but that didn't make it bad.

The male clothing consisted of loose pants and

a tunic shirt. They were big on her, but the rope belt and some inventive rolling helped them to stay on. By the time she carried her dirty plate and clothes into the main area, Alek was ready to go.

"Leave the plate and clothes on the table. I'll send someone to clean the place."

Kendall did as instructed. His curt tone and purposeful walk worried her a bit. There was no affection in him, no smiles or charm. "Alek, did I…?"

He stopped, turning his blank expression toward her.

"It's not important. Thank you for this." She gave a weak nod and moved out of the house first. He followed behind her, stopping to turn the light mirror to darken the house. He then grabbed a pack off the floor and slung it over his shoulder. He closed the house and silently led her into the forest without saying a word.

10

THE LIGHT OUTSIDE shifted and changed as they walked over the endless mountain paths. The trails snaked off in several directions, winding into the many distances. By the time they arrived at his home, Kendall knew she wouldn't be able to find her way back to the cabin. The fresh air and open scenery would have made the perfect landscape to some old Earth movie transmission sold at the Torgan marketplace. Though the air was cool, the male attire provided Kendall with enough warmth as to not be uncomfortable. If she had stayed, she might actually have asked to have the pants sewn into her size, rather than wear dresses all the time.

A strange melancholy settled over her, created by the inner war between what life on world would be like with a man like Alek, and the life she chose to go back to. It wasn't much of a choice really. How could she abandon her sister? And her father, fallen as he was, was still her father. Someone had to take care of him.

"Do you happen to have access to a time-conversion chart in your home?" Kendall took a deep breath. Her legs burned from the long mountain trek. Alek hardly seemed affected by the exercise and kept a naturally fast pace.

"Not a full chart. Mirek might have a few for when he deals with alien ambassadors. Was there a particular conversion you needed?"

"Tempastas. It's rare. I don't know why we even use it except it's what the family has always used."

"I haven't heard of it. I doubt we have access here, but we would at the palace."

"But the communication lines don't work."

"Not for a long while. The repairs are overdue. We have become too accustomed to just sending runners whenever we need to send messages. If there is time before Mirek can arrange a flight, I will send someone to find the information you require."

"Thank you." The trail turned upward. She stopped talking and breathed deeply to fight the burn in her muscles.

Conversation was stunted. At times, he would point into the forest and start talking of the birds or trees or plants, but when she inquired further his words would come to a slow stop and silence would persist once more. There was something off in his manner too. His eyes didn't meet hers and he kept a strict distance between their bodies.

"We have arrived," he stated.

Kendall blinked rapidly in surprise as he stopped. She nearly crashed into him. Stumbling back a few steps, she regained her footing and looked up at the fortress of a mountain castle. It was surrounded by steep mountains, narrow passes and rocky crags dotted with lush plant life. With its great height, how was it possible she didn't see hints of it before now? The carved façade beautifully crafted to disguise its purpose unified nature with the manmade. The rock was red with streaks of gray through the stone.

"This is Mirek's home?" she asked.

"I live here with all my brothers, though Vlad often stays in the village where he spent much of his childhood or camping in the forest." Alek raised his hand in greeting as a man came from the large rectangular structure of the ceffyl stables. "Cenek!"

"Many blessings, my lord," Cenek responded with a slight smile. "We received news of your marriage."

Alek glanced in her direction. He merely nodded at his friend. "How is the mare?"

"Is that why you came back so soon? I told the boy not to worry you. The mare is well, sad at the loss as they normally are, but I have been letting some of the young village boys sleep in the stables with her. They're in there now, making a great game of being mothered by the beast." As if to give evidence to Cenek's claim, a loud humanesque bleat sounded from inside the stables followed by the laughter of young children.

Alek sighed. "Just don't let her get too attached to them."

Cenek grinned as an answering noise came from the ceffyl inside the stables. "It might be too late."

Alek grimaced but hardly looked upset by the development. Kendall watched the interplay between the two men with interest, unsure if she should interrupt.

"Many blessings, my lady," Cenek said, acknowledging her. "Welcome home."

Kendall started to correct him but stopped herself. Instead, she said, "Thank you, my lord."

Cenek laughed. "No, not me. I'm only a ceffyl trainer. I'm no lord and would never want to be." He slapped Alek on the arm. "Imagine me, a lord."

"Lord of the ceffyls," Alek answered dryly.

"I like that." Cenek nodded. He had a gruff face, but there was the ghost of a smile that seemed to radiate from him even when it did not physically show. "Lord Mirek tells me that all brothers were blessed this year, as were the princes. I think the gods favor us and it will be a good season."

"So Mirek is here?" Kendall asked, unable to stop the question. Her stomach tightened and her heart fluttered in her chest. She didn't know what to think as she looked at Alek for a reaction, but his expression remained blank. This was what she wanted, wasn't it? To find Mirek and go home. Then why did her insides suddenly feel like the gelatinous insides of a lophibian sea slug?

"Yes. You must be eager to see Lady Riona. It's unfortunate what has happened to her," Cenek answered.

"Mirek's wife?" Alek asked, surprised.

Cenek nodded. "The lady lives. The physicians are in with her now and Mirek has sent for more. I helped the alien doctors carry in a stasis container for her. They have her in isolation while she sleeps."

"Riona is in isolation?" Kendall asked, thinking of Aeron. The woman had no idea her sister was sick. Yes, Riona was a degenerate gambler, but that didn't mean Kendall wished her harm. "What is wrong with her? Is she contagious? Will she wake up?"

"I believe it is an alien disease, my lady. I have

never heard of anything making a person sleep for so long, though they did find her in a patch of the yellow. The physicians will be able to tell you more." Cenek bowed. "If you would excuse me, my loyal subjects need ran and fed."

Kendall watched Cenek disappear inside the stables. "I hope Riona is all right. That's Aeron's sister."

"Galaxy Brides is supposed to screen for diseases." Alek led the way toward the home. Unlike the palace, there were no guards waiting to greet them at the entryway. "I'm beginning to think it's time we renegotiated our contract with them. These problems should not be arising."

"Surely it is just a precaution. What is a field of the yellow anyway?"

"The yellow plant that grows in the forest by the palace produces a spore that makes people sleep when inhaled. Though fatal in large doses, its effects do wear off rather quickly once you stop breathing it in. It doesn't cause prolonged illnesses, especially none that require physicians and isolation."

"I don't understand. You just said it could be fatal," Kendall countered.

"Only if you were to lie down in a field and no one found you for days. You would eventually starve in your sleep. However, if someone goes missing we look for them."

"Aeron said the king drugged her with a yellow plant?" Kendall looked warily at the ground. She didn't see any yellow plant life.

"Bron mentioned our uncle lost patience with her at the wedding ceremony because she became overly emotional. Since the king married a Draig woman, he is not used to the temperaments of human females. He probably thought he was calming her."

"By drugging her?"

"It's only plant spores inhaled through the nose. The effects don't last long if you don't sleep in a field of it."

"But he *drugged* her." Kendall watched Alek carefully. When it became clear he wasn't going to try to defend the king to her, she said, "Is there anything around here that I should be worried about?"

"It doesn't grow this high in the mountains," he answered. "Come, we'll find Mirek inside."

"Is there anything else besides the yellow I should know about?" She thought of their long trek through the mountains. Everything looked strange to her.

"Nothing you will be around long enough to encounter."

They walked into the shadowed entryway. Although a series of iron gates had been built to block the home from attack, they were now retracted into the stone walls. No one stopped them from entering as they made their way inside. Not wanting to fall back into the uncomfortable silence of their mountain walk, she asked, "Does Cenek live here too?"

"He sleeps here when he chooses, leaves when he chooses," Alek said. "He has a family, so unless there is a reason for him to stay he usually goes home to them. It is a short shifted run to the nearby mining community. His home is right along the edge of town in the forest."

As he led her deeper into the home, a soft light radiated from long strips in the wall. Had she not seen it for herself, she would never have believed there was such a place inside the base of a mountain nestled in a valley. The carved perfection of the hallway split into five sections. Kendall stopped, looking down each. She couldn't tell the difference between them.

Alek glanced back at her. He stood in the entrance to the fourth hall from the right. "It is quite simple to navigate the homes if you remember the birth order. Starting on the right is Bron, the oldest, then my hall. The center is the common rooms where we get together to dine, read, entertain guests or relax as a group. Then this hall is for Mirek and the last is for the youngest, Vladan. I suppose now Bron is married he will be moving into the tower rooms, as is expected. No one has been up there since my parents died."

"That doesn't sound too complicated," she said, though she wasn't as confident as she tried to sound.

"There are more passages inside each hall, but you shouldn't get too lost if you stay on the main level and don't take any stairs. The tunnels, especially below, are designed to confuse intruders. The outer halls spiral outward in a maze-like pattern to trap those unfamiliar with our system. Should the interior be breached, any attackers would be dispersed into the sides of the mountain until they can be found and dealt with. If you go down a path and are not able to open a door once we scan you into the main system, you are heading down a dead end and should turn around. Though I suppose you won't be scanned into the system. I would teach you the rest, but..."

"I'm not going to be here long," she finished quietly when he wouldn't.

"Yes," he said, his manner becoming stiff once more. "It would be best if you didn't wander about alone."

"I want every test run twice, no, three times.

Make sure nothing is left to chance." The sound of an urgent male voice filled Mirek's hall before a Draig man emerged behind two very pristinely dressed physicians. The two doctors were not native to the planet and had Medical Alliance insignia on their long jackets. One carried a small container in front of him with gloved hands. The other clicked her finger against an electronic clipboard as she walked. The Draig man, who could only be Mirek, continued, "This is my wife and I will spend every space credit or ore shipment I have to ensure her health. Anything you can tell me about her condition—*anything*—you contact me immediately."

"Lord Mirek, we always do a thorough job," the doctor with the clipboard answered. She was all business and didn't even bother to turn around from what she was doing. The man beside her paused, glancing back with a reassuring smile as he waited to fall into step next to Mirek.

"The best thing you can do is keep her inside the…" the male doctor began, only to stop when he saw Alek and Kendall.

"It's fine, he's family," Mirek prompted, his words rushed.

"Keep her in the stasis unit until an isolation room can be built. I will personally see to it the plans are sent down as soon as we're back on our ship." The male doctor smiled. The female doctor kept walking, not bothering to look up from her work as she passed Kendall. Not wanting to get trampled, Kendall stepped back out of her way and leaned against the stone wall. The male doctor rushed after his rude companion.

"Mirek, you married?" Alek asked when the doctors had left. "When? Your stone did not glow at the ceremony."

"Wait," Kendall said, hurrying after the doctors. "I need to ask you something."

Both doctors stopped and turned to her. The woman arched an icy brow. "Well?"

Kendall held up her hand. "Tracking chip. I need it disabled."

The female doctor let loose a long, irritated sigh. She tapped her clipboard and then held her hand out. Kendall placed her hand in the doctor's. The woman jerked her forward, pressed her palm down on the clipboard. A tiny red light glowed beneath Kendall's hand in the webbing between her thumb and forefinger.

"Scalpel." The woman held her hand out to her colleague.

Kendall flinched as the man gave the other doctor a laser scalpel and no anesthetic. Instead of cutting her, the doctor turned the scalpel upside down and slammed it hard against the red light.

Kendall yelped as pain shot through her hand. The light had disappeared.

"Scar tissue will take care of the rest. I'll add it to your bill." The woman slid the clipboard away from Kendall and continued on down the hall. Her companion hurried behind her.

"Ow," Kendall breathed, cradling her hand to her chest. The red mark would surely form a bruise later.

Mirek glanced at Kendall. He had the same medium brown hair that seemed to run in the family, but his eyes were bright green. Should she venture a guess by his haggard expression, she would say this man hadn't slept for days. His eyes looked tired, not that she knew what his eyes normally looked like.

"My bride missed the receiving line. I think she was held up, or lost, or something." Mirek said, answering Alek's early question. He glanced behind him, clearly indicating by his anxious movements that he wanted to get back to his bride.

Alek took the hint and walked with his brother down the hall. Kendall stayed behind them, holding her injured hand, and let the men talk. She couldn't understand what they were saying as they spoke in their native tongue.

The brothers had the same long gait and purposeful strides. It was easy to tell they'd grown up in the same home. The hall turned and curved, twisting its way through the mountain. They stayed on a steady course, but Kendall felt lost by the time they reached Mirek's home. Mirek ran his hand over an intricately carved door frame and stated, "Open." The wooden door glided open and he led them inside.

Mirek's section of the mountain home had smoothed stone floors, thick rugs and oversized wood furniture. A banner of a dragon standard hung on the wall. Its prominent placement and large size gave away its importance.

Couches were arranged in a square around a low table with a center fire pit. The only thing out of place was the stasis unit sitting on one of the couches. The large plastic crate was more service-able than decorative. She guessed that was where Riona rested. For some reason, she hesitated as the men went to the stasis unit. Mirek placed his hand gingerly on top as if he might hurt the woman inside by pressing too hard on the transparent lid. Alek looked in and said nothing for a long moment.

Kendall could not see Riona from where she stood, but she didn't want to get closer. The stasis unit reminded her of her own captivity. Her hands trembled at the idea of being carted around in a plastic crate like cargo. The clear lid would let anyone who wanted to look in at her. What had happened while she was locked away? Was she shown to buyers before Galaxy Brides took her? Was she put on auction? Was she dressed or naked? The not knowing was perhaps the worst part of the whole ordeal.

But this moment wasn't about her. It was about Mirek and Riona. Kendall tried to hide her trembling as she slowly joined the men by the couch. Riona's eyes were closed in what Kendall determined to be forced sleep. Even if whatever sleeping sickness she had had disappeared, the medicines in the booth would keep the woman from waking up. It would be for the best. If she woke up, she'd be in pain if the look of her skin was any indication. Red patches of blisters created strange patterns on the woman's flesh. Around those bumps the skin was pale, too pale for the healthy Riona she remembered on the ship. The auburn length of her hair had been pulled and twisted on the top of her head into a very neat, very plain bun. A tube filled with yellow liquid stuck out of her side. A fine powder coated her skin. It was what made her look so pale.

"You need to tell her sister," Kendall said quietly.

Alek touched her arm. "Everything that can be done will be done."

"She's been asleep since the wedding ceremony. I can't wake her up. I brought her here to receive medical attention. The stasis unit is to keep her comfortable while she sleeps. We don't know if she is in pain. The doctors have never seen anything like it. At best, they think she might have had an allergic reaction to something on the planet."

"And at worst?" Alek asked.

"That she carries a plague. Don't worry. I have been tested and no one who has been around her is sick. She is stable, but for now it is best if she breathes filtered air. I called in several favors to have this stasis pod delivered." Mirek caressed the transparent lid, as if tracing his wife's face. Kendall studied him, noting the openness of his raw expression. There was longing in him, and frustration, and concern. The emotions radiated from his features. "The builders will start construction on a special isolation room for her just as soon as the supplies can be delivered. I have sent for more doctors and a new medic unit with all the upgraded technology. I'm not hopeful it will do much, as the medical booths we currently have are not that old and they are not helping her."

Kendall glanced to her husband. His face was always so guarded compared to the emotion Mirek showed for his sleeping wife. The two of them couldn't have known each other long since Riona had arrived on the Galaxy Bride ship and, by the sounds of it, was passed out by the following morning. Kendall wondered what it was about her own husband that made him so stubborn, so shielded.

She wanted to reach out and touch Alek's face so she could search deep in his eyes. Maybe the answers she sought would be there. Or perhaps it was better not to know since she was leaving. Alek met her searching gaze and nodded. As if resigned, he said to Mirek, "I know the timing is unfortunate, but my wife needs a ride to…" He glanced at her expectantly.

"X Quadrant," she supplied. "Roaming Fueling Station at the X's Deep Space Port registered to lot X-65J."

Mirek gave her a strange look. "Roaming Fueling Station?"

"My family is there," she answered.

He nodded. "If you don't mind parting with some of your personal ore supply, there is a vessel that will make the trip. It's an older ship I added to the fleet about ten years ago in trade. It's been reconditioned, but I have to warn you the luxury leaves a little to be desired. It's pretty fast, but takes a lot of fuel to run the long trips."

"What about the newer ships?" Alek asked.

"None of the pilots currently certified for those vessels are nearby. Don't look so worried, brother, the ship is older but sturdy." Mirek slapped his brother's arm. "It'll fly you straight, and the pilot might be new but he's well trained."

Alek didn't look comforted.

"You're lucky we even have a pilot who is free to take you. The other pilots are scattered about the mountains with their families. Since we had the Breeding Festival I did not have any scheduled ambassadorial trips. I'll have it readied for you both by morning."

"Both?" Kendall asked, curious.

"I assume you would want your family to meet your husband," Mirek said. "I trust the men manning the flight, but I don't trust the port stops along the way should something happen. Some aliens do not respect a female who travels alone. As my sister, I cannot allow you to go unescorted."

It was an old-fashioned concept of chivalry, but she found herself not protesting. If it would give her a few more days with Alek, she would take them. She wasn't ready to say goodbye yet.

"If he wants to come," Kendall answered.

Mirek nodded as if Alek's travel plans were a foregone conclusion. "Then it is settled."

Alek didn't answer.

11

ALEK LED the way through Mirek's hall. Not going the way they had come, as evidenced by the new tapestries Kendall saw hanging on the walls, but rather through a long maze of hallways and doors. He opened the doors with a hand scanner. She watched the doors slide closed behind them, trapping her with Alek deep in the mountain's core. Though she wasn't really worried by the fact. She trusted Alek as a man of his word. If he was going to harm her, he would have done it already.

"I didn't realize you would have to travel with me. I'm sorry if I put you in an awkward position with your family," Kendall said, trying to fill the silence. In truth, she wasn't sorry. She wanted him to go with her.

"It is what is expected," he answered, not

sounding surprised or put out by the notion of leaving his planet. Then again, he was always so serious. There were glimpses of emotion, but nothing like the display Mirek had shown. Come to think of it, nothing like Bron had shown either. She wondered why her husband had become so guarded with himself. Perhaps if she had more time she would learn his secrets.

"Have you ever been off planet?" she asked.

"Yes. As children we were expected to go into orbit to get a feel for it, and I have joined Mirek a handful of times over the years on his ambassadorial missions. Though, those trips were only to take a shuttle up to meet an alien ship in our airspace." He kept walking. She wanted to touch him, to make him stop. More than that, she wanted to kiss him, to have him press her up against the wall and make love to her like he had next to the cabin.

"Have you ever left orbit? Have you been to deep space?"

He stopped walking and turned to her. "No. There has never been a need."

The very idea seemed foreign to her. Never seeing deep space? Living on one planet…forever?

"Open," Alek commanded. She stopped in surprise before realizing he spoke to the central computer hidden in the stone. A door opened and he moved aside so she could step into the room first. "This is my home, *our* home for the brief time you are here. Relax. Eat. Look about. I have nothing to hide." He didn't follow her in. "I will be back later. I must speak to my brother about the arrangements for our trip."

Before Kendall could answer, the door slid shut and he was gone. Alek's home was nothing like Mirek's. The layout was different, as was the décor. Though for the most part clean, piles of clutter were strewn over tables and chairs. A row of stairs disappeared into an upper level.

Leather straps connected to pieces of metal were placed over the back of a thickly stuffed couch. She'd seen similar items hanging in the stables at the palace. The couch faced a barren fire pit.

A wood table was inset into the wall with bench seats. Stacks of papers and electronic devices lined its top. On the walls hung a dragon standard much like the wall at Mirek's. However, there were also woven tapestries depicting birds and forest creatures—some large and fierce, others gentle and small. She slowly made her way toward the table. A door led to a bathing room. Another opened to a wide space with weapons on the wall and little else. Yet another led to a kitchen set up similar to the cabin home. She stopped at the table and looked down.

Electronic clipboards were turned off and labeled with the Qurilixen language. She didn't have the necessary upload to be able to translate what the labels said. Rolled parchments were stacked in the corner and flat parchments were stretched out before one of the seats. When she sat on the bench, she pulled the flat parchment toward her and lifted a blank piece. Beneath the paper were several drawings. The sketches had been done by hand with a primitive drawing instrument. The black lines were bold with delicate degrees of shading to fill in the contours. Almost all of the drawings were of nature—trees and forest paths, ceffyl mothers with their babies, the mountains, birds and forest creatures much like the ones on his tapestries. There were a few pictures of children playing, one of Cenek, some of Alek's brothers. If these belonged to Alek, the man had a great talent for detail.

Kendall traced one of the lines with her finger. Alek did not draw himself into his pictures. Then, coming to the very last page, she found the ceremonial valley of tents from the Breeding Ceremony as if seen from a high angle. The layout was different than she remembered seeing, but the wilted leaves on the trees and the darker shading gave the hint of one night of darkness on the planet.

In a surreal way, the images painted a story of

Alek's life. They were serene yet isolated, powerful yet sad in their solitary lines. They were images she would never get to see with him, the secrets of the planet that would be left behind in the morning.

ALEK LET LOOSE a long breath as he strode away from his wing back to his brother's home. Being near Kendall was hard. He wanted to touch her, but to do so would only cause him more pain. One kiss and he would be begging her to stay with him when she had made it very clear she'd never wanted to be on his planet.

"Are you going to come inside, or are you going to stand by my door brooding," Mirek said from within his home.

Alek commanded the door to open and stepped in.

Mirek sat by his wife's stasis unit, his hand on top of her plastic crate—the only way he could hold her in her condition. "I see you chose to come inside and brood."

"I don't want our brothers to know I've left," Alek said. "They have enough to worry about without thinking of me in deep space."

Mirek arched a brow.

"Bron's marriage should be settled, but it is not settled well." Alek sighed. "And mine…"

"The trip isn't so you can meet her family, is it?" Mirek absently traced circles over his wife's still form. "I suspected as much by the look on your bride's face when I suggested you go with her." He gave a short, humorless laugh. "You are welcome for that by the way. Whatever is happening between you, this should give you more time with her."

"If you wanted to give me more time you could have been a little less accommodating with the ship."

"You asked for a ride so I granted it. Without knowing the details I did not think it best to delay her departure in case it was an emergency, but the least I could do is to give you a chance to fix whatever is broken by sending you along."

"I am afraid our marriages are cursed," Alek said. "Bron was unable to resist his bride and consummated the marriage early." He quickly told Mirek about Bron's capture, the possible alien threat, the possible dissatisfaction of the gods. "And I did not follow ceremony as I should have and now my bride is set to leave me. You did not find your bride in the receiving line and she lies here like this. Perhaps this is a sign that our bloodline is to die. Vladan, as our adopted brother, will continue the family name and traditions."

"The Tyoe are aggressive in their dealings," Mirek said. "They tried to buy our mines and offered an insulting price because they assumed we were barbaric and stupid. I refused as I always do. They are not the only aliens to covet our ore. That is the price to pay for such a profitable industry. Though, honestly, their offer was better than those who try to get us to do all the labor while they reap the profits. I doubt there is anything worth finding, but if Bron's bride suspects them to be a threat, I will look into it. There are ways of tracking whether or not ships have been in our airspace. Most crafts leave behind a residual energy that can be detected. That should tell us whether Bron's capture was alien or local."

"Var, aliens or the gods. I'm not sure which option is the worst fate," Alek said.

Mirek studied his wife's still face. Riona didn't move. Alek had a hard time looking at the poor woman with the tube sticking in her side.

"I cannot believe all hope is lost. We aren't bad people, Alek. We don't deserve this. I must believe that the gods test us, nothing more, and that all will be well if we are strong." Mirek leaned over and placed a kiss on the transparent lid before standing. "Come, let us find a drink."

"Always the optimist."

"Hardly." Mirek went to his wall and opened a hidden latch. The panel revealed a supply of rum. Taking a bottle and two goblets, he poured the thick liquid and sat down at the rounded table. He took a long drink before refilling his goblet.

Alek joined him but didn't touch the liquor. "I promised Kendall I would get her home if she agreed to marry me."

Mirek froze. "I can only imagine how hard it is for you to admit that to me."

"I will honor my word and take her home."

"Why does she want to go home?" Mirek asked. "What is there for her?"

"She…" Alek paused. He'd never actually asked her specifically why. She kept insisting that she needed to go home and so he was taking her home.

"She did not tell you and you did not ask." Mirek shook his head. "There is a reason you are not the diplomat in the family, my brother. You think everything can be said in silence and gestures. I am your blood and I sometimes cannot guess what you are thinking."

"I am not so closed," he protested.

"You are not so open. Your stubbornness keeps you from saying anything resembling emotions. There are years I think you say more to your ceffyls than you do to your brothers. Women are not like beasts, Alek, and they are not like us. Your wife has not known you as long as we have."

"I do not treat my wife as a ceffyl." Alek

lowered his tone in warning. He did not like his brother implying otherwise.

"Maybe you should." Mirek was tired, that much was obvious, but he was also unconcerned with Alek's temper. "A little softness in her direction wouldn't hurt the situation. You stood by her like a statue, barely looking at her, while she could barely keep her eyes off you. The gods would not have sent you a woman who was incapable of dealing with that stubborn streak of yours in the long term, but you have got to give the woman a chance to know you before it's too late and she is gone forever."

Alek clenched his hands around the goblet of rum. He had shown her more emotion than he had anyone else in his life. He had married her, which had to speak volumes about what he felt. His crystal had glowed for her. He showed her he wanted her with his kisses and touch. How could there be doubt as to what he wanted, what he felt?

"If you continue to be stubborn, you will lose her. Your bride is before you, breathing and alive. If you don't fight for her with every weapon you have, and that includes making yourself vulnerable, you don't deserve to keep her and the gods will be right in taking her from you." Mirek took Alek's full goblet from him and helped himself to the liquor. Then, setting the empty goblet down, he said, "I will not tell the others of your journey unless it becomes necessary. I'm surprised Bron gave you direct orders to repair the communications. Of all things for him to use his title on, that seems an odd choice. If he wanted you at the cabin, he should have just ordered you to stay at the cabin. He must have realized it was an impossible task. You didn't have the supplies or the training necessary to do the job. Bron knows you're better suited to nature than electronics. I wonder what he was thinking."

"I couldn't find the control panel." Alek thought of his grandfather's treasure, but said nothing about it. He wasn't in the mood to brag or reminisce. The liquor would still be there after he dropped off his wife. "Isn't it in the walls somewhere?"

"No, I don't think so. Isn't it in the forest? Or buried underground?" Mirek frowned. "There should be plans somewhere."

"One would imagine."

Mirek waved a dismissing hand. "The ship you take is not needed here. Cenek has the ceffyls well in hand. I will handle the communication repairs by getting the workers started on it. While they are there, I will have men listening to the forest for changes. There is no reason for you to rush back. I cannot make the ship fly slower and risk the others guessing as to the reason for it, but I can make it unnecessary for you to come back too quickly. The crew will not expect you to be in a hurry to leave a meeting with her family."

"I did defy the duke's order," Alek said, slightly sarcastically.

Mirek chuckled, the first real expression of amusement Alek had seen since coming home. "Best not to tell him. If he does find out, all the more reason for you to be in deep space."

"If I come back with Kendall, it will be worth it. If I come back alone, nothing he can do to me will match the pain I will be feeling." Alek slowly stood.

Mirek eyed him in shock. "That is the most I have ever heard you admit about your... Did you say as much to your wife?"

Alek stiffened, not knowing how to answer. Instead, he diverted the subject. "If you have Riona's medical records uploaded to the ship computer, I will see what I can find out about your wife's illness. Someone in the high skies must know what it is."

Alek was almost sorry he'd mentioned it. His brother's eyes moved to the couch and the light went out of them. Mirek lacked patience, and having to wait for his bride to wake up would be the worst kind of torture. His expression and his manners tightened. "Thank you, but I have already sent the necessary inquiries."

Alek touched his brother's shoulder briefly. There was nothing he could say to ease Mirek's suffering. Riona was ill. No words, no professing of love or emotions could help change that fact. The lack of such brotherly professions wouldn't bother Mirek.

Mirek grabbed Alek's hand when he would pull it away. "I smell the nef on you, brother. I don't know where you got it, or how, but don't take it. Don't numb yourself to your bride while she stands before you. Perhaps that is why the gods send you into space. There are reasons for things, though I do not claim to know them."

Alek reached into his pocket and took out the small bottle of nef he'd taken from the treasure trove of liquor at the cabin. He set it on the table before Mirek. There was no point in denying his shame in having contemplated taking the drug to ease his burden. "I only tasted it. I didn't drink it."

"A taste is enough, I've heard," Mirek said. "I can smell it on you so some must have gotten into your system. Go find your bride and work it out."

Alek left Mirek's home to search out his own. He knew he should heed his brother's advice and say something to Kendall, but he wasn't sure how to start. Blurting out something like, "I need you so you can't leave me or I will die," seemed a bit dramatic, and yet that is how he felt. Ceffyls seemed to sense his emotions and he theirs. With a woman? Alek thought he sensed her. The over-whelming pain he'd felt inside her had been very, very real. Surely she could sense how strongly he felt for her?

When Alek entered his home it was to find Kendall standing near the kitchen door holding her sleeve over her nose. She breathed hard. Her eyes met his in a near panic.

"What is it?" he asked, hurrying inside. He partially shifted but couldn't sense anything wrong.

"I'm cooking," she mumbled against her shirt.

Alek went to the kitchen. Meat was laid out on the counter with a few uneven strips cut off and thrown into a pan. The pan smoked and the food was almost to the point of burning.

"The smell." She backed away from the door. "I can't take the smell. It's too…" As if to prove her point, she coughed and gagged into her sleeve. "That can't be what cooking food is supposed to smell like."

Alek hurriedly took the pan off the fire and set it aside.

"I thought I could handle it this time, but I don't know why it is. I had the same reaction when Aeron prepared meat. It's so potent." She didn't move her sleeve. "I'm sorry. I know it's your custom to prepare meals yourself, but would you happen to have a food simulator hidden somewhere?"

Alek came out of the kitchen and went to a wall next to the table. "Mirek had them installed in case we had visiting dignitaries to entertain with special diet requirements. I never actually used it." He ran his hand over the panel. The unit was set into the wall. "He sends someone in to update the menus, but I can barely remember how it works. There should be a menu code list somewhere with programming directions."

"I don't think I've ever seen this model, but they're all pretty standard," Kendall said, dropping her arm. She sighed in relief as the smell dissipated. "I had one similar to this on the fueling dock." He watched as she activated it and began typing on the panel without instructions. Within seconds she was pulling out a plate of steaming food and a pronged utensil. She took a deep breath and gave a slight smile. "I can't believe you still have this menu code in there. They took tomato basil pasta out of the newer units and our old one was hawked for parts to pay —it doesn't matter. Apparently old Earth menus are no longer fashionable." She took a deep breath, having no problem with the smell of the simulator's cooked dish. He sniffed. It lacked the freshness he was used to and the scent was light, barely there.

"I haven't had this since I was a kid. My father told me that it was my mother's favorite, so it's all I would eat."

"You don't remember your mother for yourself?" This was the first time she'd offered information about her parents. Usually she would try to change the topic whenever her father came up. He'd let her, assuming she would tell him what she wanted him to know.

"She died when I was born. I'm told I look nothing like her." She gave a small shrug. "It's sad, but I'm used to it. All I have are the stories my father told me about her. She was a traveling saleswoman who lived a very ordinary life. They met on the fueling dock. She never left. It's the same way he met Margot's mother."

"I've heard you say this name before, Margot." Alek moved his papers aside on the tabletop to make room for her, then looked at the food simulator and frowned.

"Do you want to try this?"

He really didn't. The plate of pale string and red chunks hardly looked appealing and the smell was bland. Alek found himself politely answering, "Yes, thank you," if only to please her by taking the offered dish that meant so much to her. The gesture was out of character for him and took him a bit by surprise. When he was seated across from her, he watched her stab and twirl the dining utensil so that the strings wrapped around it. He mimicked her movements, trying a small bite. It tasted strange, not horrible, but strange enough to make him take a second bite. He tried to place the moist texture but it was unlike anything he'd eaten before. "Margot? She is your sister?"

She nodded. "Yes. Her mother also died in childbirth. It's not as suspicious as it sounds, two women dying in childbirth in this star era, at least not when you don't have access to a medical unit. I helped raise Margot. My father didn't have the mind to remember feeding times and schoolwork."

Instead of taking a third bite, he set the utensil down. The pain of her leaving did not lessen, but he now saw the honor in it. "I understand."

Kendall gave him a quizzical look. "What do you understand?"

"That is why you must go back. You are this girl's mother and you are concerned she is not being fed as often as a child should. I respect your privacy, but I wish you would have told me sooner so that I might have understood the true urgency of your situation. I take it she's young?"

"Yes." Kendall nodded. "About twelve years by the tempastas time chart. From what I understand, most alien calendars track age by roughly the same cycle. But I would not say I am her mother. I am simply her sister."

"A sister who acts in place of her mother. The feelings in that situation are much the same, I would imagine." Alek didn't touch the stringy food again. Kendall toyed with her meal, pushing the red chunks around to form a smiling face before mixing them into the pasta. "Will your father not watch out for her? In your absence, will he not take on his proper duties?"

"My father is ill."

"And you must care for him as well? Does he have long?"

"My father suffers from…" She paused and stabbed a red piece a little too hard. "He gambles. Quite a bit. He also loses quite a bit. Some call that an illness. Some call it a weakness. I call it reality." Bitterness seeped into her tone. "He once lost part of our security camera circuitry. He lost six months' worth of food simulator cells. He lost an entire fuel shipment, which is just as bad as losing the cells as we had no money to buy more food with no fuel to sell. He lost most of my mother's jewels and Margot's mother's valuables. He lost my inheritance from my mother, meager as it was. He once lost an entire length of catwalk grating and we were unable to rent half of our private rooms to travelers until I bartered for a replacement. If it can be gambled, he will lose it."

"And you," Alek said quietly, everything coming together. "He lost you. That is what the repossession was all about, wasn't it?"

Kendall nodded, not meeting his gaze. He felt her pain wash over him again. "Yes. Apparently, it wasn't the first time he used me as collateral. Only this time he was unable to turn his losing streak back around. They collected me to pay for his debts and I was sold to Galaxy Brides as cargo. I barely remember anything between the repossession agents coming to claim me and waking on the Galaxy Brides ship. I was kept as cargo in stasis. There were moments when I would wake up between containers, or when they put me in medical booths. The time blurs together like a hazy dream I can't quite pick apart."

"Your father did not act honorably." He was unsure how to comfort her, but he desperately wanted to. What did a husband say to such a thing?

"Thank you." She nodded, seeming to understand his sentiment and take some comfort from it.

This was a sense of obligation Alek could understand and respect, even if he couldn't relate to it. He nodded. "You are right, of course. Helping him is the honorable thing."

"I know you don't think my worrying is very

honorable, but I have to go back before he loses Margot, before he loses the fueling dock, before he has nothing left to give them and they put him in debtors' prison or take his life. Flawed as he is, he is my father and I must help him."

"What do you mean that is what I think?" The very thought of her believing that left him cold.

"At the cabin. You said worrying wasn't honorable."

"About your husband's worth, not all worries," he corrected. "I apologize if you misunderstood me. Is that how you really think of me? That hard?"

She didn't meet his gaze.

Alek was unsure how to explain himself better. "Would your father consider coming here to live?"

Kendall shook her head in denial. "No. I wouldn't want to do that to you or your family, and there is no way he will leave that fueling dock. Thank you, though, for listening and for the offer."

As much as Alek wanted to force her father to come back to Qurilixen, he understood well the stubbornness that could drive people. His own father would never have left his home world had the situation been reversed. Short of kidnapping the man and keeping him under constant guard for the rest of his life, there was little Alek could do but try to convince him to move. In light of her words,

Kendall did not seem so unwilling to be with him, but rather it was her duty that called her away. As a man of honor, he understood duty. His duty to his family kept him where he lived. So, instead of convincing Kendall to stay, he would convince her father to leave the fueling dock.

"I wish I could abandon him," she whispered. "But if I do I might as well kill him myself. It would amount to the same thing. I know I shouldn't care after all he's done, but he's not all bad. There is some good mixed in with the flaws."

"These matters are complicated." Alek nodded in agreement. "The ship is being readied and we will board in the morning."

"Thank you." She pushed her plate forward and stood from the table. He watched her as she came to stand by him. For a moment, her hand hesitated before reaching to touch his face. "I looked at your artwork. You're very talented."

Alek glanced over to the stack of parchment on the table. The top page was blank but he knew the drawings she spoke of. "It eases the boredom."

"You're very talented," she repeated.

"Thank you."

"I wouldn't have guessed you were an artist. I wonder what else you do that I wouldn't have guessed at." Kendall trailed the tip of her finger down the slope of his nose. "You are a very hard man to read, Alek." She traced his eyebrows. "With Bron and Mirek it is easy to guess what they are thinking." She moved her finger to his lips. The light touch held his attention. He didn't move to touch her, merely looked up at her as she stood next to his seat. "What happened to you growing up that makes you so different from your brothers?"

"I don't know that anything happened. As children, Bron was the spoiled future high duke. Mirek was the baby. I somehow became the quiet one stuck between them. My mother used to tell me that I didn't even cry when I was born. Then Vladan was adopted into our family after his parents died in a mining accident. He was the wild one, raised outside our nobility."

"What happened to your parents?" She ran her fingers over his lips as she spoke, tracing the edges.

"An alien illness stole their years. They went on an ambassadorial mission. The aliens naturally carried a plague virus we are susceptible to. It was one of those strange and unexplainable accidents. The aliens meant no harm. Now all Draig are inoculated against it when they are born. My parents died quickly and together."

"I'm sorry you lost them. It must not be easy to have memories of them to haunt you," she said.

"It must not be easy to have no memory of your mother at all," he answered.

She nodded. She slid her hand to his neck and tangled her fingers in the hair at his nape. Alek moved his hands to rest on her hips. She drew slowly closer to him, caught in the contemplative mood that settled between them.

"I am sorry I accused you of scheming to force me to stay. I have been so worried about my sister. I don't want to forget to thank you for all you have done for me. You saved me from repossession, kept me safe on your planet, fed me, sheltered me and now you are helping me to get home. None of these were your burden to take on. Without your interference, I would have been resold on another planet and it might not have turned out so well for me. I owe you a lot, Alek. More than can be repaid. But I at least want you to let me pay your family back for the cost of the trip. Without knowing the state of the fueling dock, I can't say when I will be able to come up with enough space credits, but doing so will be my priority."

"Whether you are here or in space, you are my wife, Kendall." He didn't like the thought of not having her, but having anyone else was an impossibility for him. "Distance will not change that. You will have a home here. What is mine is yours. So you owe me nothing."

Her sadness washed over him, but beneath the grief was a longing he well understood. It was the same emotion pumping through his veins, the desire, the yearning, the almost desperate need to change reality into something better.

"That is very sweet," she said, "but I've heard you speak of your longer life spans. I do not want you living alone. I'll give you whatever you need from me for a divorce."

The words clearly didn't bring her pleasure, yet the mere thought of them hurt him all the same.

"There are ways to break a marriage for you, but not for me," he said. "What is done will remain done."

"I can't believe that your family would want you to be alone because we were not able to be together." She again touched his face. He liked the gentleness in her, the soft feminine glide of her fingers. He was used to the firm skin of a ceffyl or the hard, brief touch of his brothers. To feel a woman's softness was intoxicating. He would miss it terribly if he lost her.

"It is not family, but the will of the gods."

"I can't believe that the gods would want you to be alone." She shook her head. "Haven't the gods ever made mistakes?"

"When we married, I put my future happiness in your hands." He took her hands in his and studied the dark bruise where the doctor had struck her. It went a long way to proving she wasn't a spy.

She didn't want to be tracked from space. Not that Alek needed proof to know she wasn't a spy. "I did so willingly and freely. I gave you that part of myself. Who am I to take it back now? That part of my life is yours. There will never be anyone else for me as long as I live—not in my bed or in my heart." He wasn't sure why he told her. His brain whispered to keep quiet, to not put that kind of guilt on her when she could not help her situation. Yet somehow Mirek's advice found its way to his tongue. It wasn't the outpouring of emotion Mirek would have suggested, but for him the explanation he gave was a big step. "I know I can appear to be…"

"Stubborn? Hard-headed?" she supplied with a small laugh and even smaller smile.

She was teasing him, but still he answered, "Yes, both of those things."

"You are also honorable and a good person." Kendall again reached for his head and pulled her fingers lightly in his hair as if she studied the locks.

"I will do everything I can to protect and help you. Whether it is today or in a hundred years, I am your husband. I have given you my life, Kendall."

A tear slid from her eye and she blinked heavily. Kendall pulled away from him and he reluctantly let her go. She turned her back on him.

Alek stood, unsure what to do. "I did not mean to upset you."

"I am so sorry. Had I known what you were giving up to help me, I wouldn't have let you do it." When she turned back to look at him, her eyes were torn between sadness and anger. "I can't believe how many lives my father's gambling has ruined. Not just directly, but the rippling aftereffects of his actions."

"Your leaving does not have to be forever. When the time comes, you may return." Alek would not wish harm on her father, but death was an eventual reality for them all. "Until such a time, I will be with you. I don't know how it will work over the length of a galaxy, but if you try you may be able to feel me and I you. Plus, we could set up communications. I could travel to visit you and you me. There are ways."

"I would like very much to remain in contact, but I worry that might almost be worse." Kendall sighed and closed her eyes. "I've gathered enough to know you'll probably outlive me by several hundred years. I'm human, Alek. In a hundred years I'll be long dead—unless you were to put me back into stasis to preserve me, but that is no life."

"Our fates are intertwined. Here, on this planet, with the aid of our blue sun you would live longer. That is true now, and when you come back." Alek didn't move, unsure what he could say or do to erase her pain. The elders believed that by claiming her as his wife and thus giving her his life, he'd shortened his years to extend hers. Without the aid of radiation from the blue sun, her life would play out like normal, maybe extended by a few more years. In the past, scientists had tried to identify the exact combination of elements to reproduce the life-giving effects of their world, but they had been unsuccessful.

Like the rest of the Draig, he was a warrior, a fighter, used to the action of doing what needed to be done. But in this situation there was no giant fanged yorkin to hunt, no Var army to battle. There was only reality and the flawed nature of imperfect men.

His wife was so lovely, so delicate. Alek wanted to protect her, to wipe the sadness from her eyes. Desire rose up inside him. Her lips parted and she inhaled, as if she sensed the moment his passion for her heated.

She again came back into his arms. He wrapped his hands around her waist to hold her there. She glided her finger down his nose. "I like when your eyes change like that. It's like your soul is spinning around in them."

When he would answer her lips stopped him. Her kiss was sweet and soft, even as her tongue swept along his mouth. The feel of her captivated all his senses until nothing mattered but that most perfect moment. He pulled her body closer, sliding forward on the seat and parting his legs so she could stand between them. When they couldn't get close enough, he stood. The angle of the kiss changed.

Alek lifted her off the ground and walked toward the stairs that would take them to his bed. Pleasure pumped through his veins. She moaned against his mouth, holding on to his neck as he carried her easily to the top level of his home. He let her inside him, not caring if she felt his emotions. Nothing else mattered, only Kendall. Through the haze of their passion everything around them faded into nothingness.

When he reached the top, he set her down on the bed and instantly crawled over her. He molded his body to hers, careful to keep his weight from crushing her yet close enough he could feel every curve of her soft flesh. Sex with his wife had always been passionate, but this time felt different. It wasn't just the desperation of the morning to come, but a closeness that had not been there before. They'd shared themselves in words and now they were enhancing those words with their bodies.

She moved her hands over him, tugging at his clothes. He maneuvered to allow her to pull his tunic over his head. Within seconds, they were stripped of their clothing. Hands glided over flesh. Mouths teased and kissed. Tongues poked and licked.

Wanting to explore her more fully, Alek rolled onto his back, taking her with him. She straddled his waist and continued kissing him. He touched everywhere he could reach, leaving no measure of skin neglected. Kendall slid her hand down his chest and along his side before reaching between their bodies to stroke his arousal. He tensed beneath her and let loose a small groan of approval.

He slid his tongue into her mouth, deepening the kiss, moving from sweet to passionate. When he could wait no longer, he flipped her onto her back and pushed at her inner thighs. She spread her legs willingly, and he didn't hesitate as he entered her. If he could have consumed her and kept her with him forever, he would have. Instead, he settled for the press of her naked body, the moist heat of her sex, the soft catches of breath in her throat.

Her nipples brushed over his chest as he moved inside her, their tight peaks drawing trails over his skin. Every detail of her impassioned expression was open to him in the dim bedroom light. He kept the pace slow, not wanting to rush their climax. Each passing second only added to the desperation.

He didn't want it to be over, didn't want to leave the moment.

Nature would not be denied and the primal search for release was finally met when she tensed and trembled beneath him. It was too much to resist. Alek found his release deep inside her.

Her legs fell limply along his and she gave a small, sated laugh. Looking up at him through lidded eyes, she whispered, "Hayo."

"Hayo?"

She gave another small laugh. "It means 'hey, you' or 'hello, you'."

"Oh." He returned her smile before kissing her softly. "Greetings, you."

"Greeyo," she answered, then laughed harder. "Never mind, that doesn't sound right, does it?"

How could he resist her relaxed humor? Chuckling, he pulled out of her body and settled on the bed next to her. It was too early for sleep but he had no intention of leaving her side. "Perhaps something that came from the backside of a yorkin."

"Yorkin?"

"Did you see the giant fanged beast depicted on the tapestry downstairs?" he asked. She nodded. "That is a yorkin."

"That's real?"

"Yes, it roams the mountains."

Kendall shivered. "But *we* are in the mountains. When I asked about the yellow plants you said there was nothing up here that… You mean that thing is…?"

Alek hugged her closer, stopping her from sitting up. "Don't worry. Yorkins do not attack here. You must travel farther north to the cave systems."

She settled in his arms. Her legs stirred, adjusting gently until finding the perfect position against him. Alek flexed his arm, holding her close. When he closed his eyes, he focused on the rhythmic rise and fall of her chest. He heard her heart beat. Before meeting her, he'd never realized just how lonely his life had been.

"I love you, Kendall. I don't want you to leave me," he whispered, knowing she'd fallen asleep. She made a light humming noise in the back of her throat but didn't answer.

Despite Mirek's insistence that the ship was older and not used often, the medium-sized craft looked to be a fine machine. The metal body was sturdy, not pretty as far as ships go, but solid. Thick strips of flashing lights lined the body, blinking slowly as the wings were extended forward fully and then retracted back into the ship's body in pre-flight tests.

Kendall glanced at Alek, who watched the final preparations. She wasn't sure if his rapt attention was from fear for their safety or because he did not come to this area of his castle home often and thus the performance was a novelty.

After making love to her again when they woke up, Alek left only to return with clothes and food. They'd dressed and eaten in relative silence. She wasn't sure what to say to him that hadn't already been said. Alek had then led her toward the mountain's base through a series of tunnels and up long stairways. Even with his longer stride and naturally faster pace, it took about fifteen minutes to reach the landing platform where the ship was being prepped.

The dress she wore was simple compared to some she'd seen worn by Draig women at the bridal ceremony, but the fabric was soft and it fit her rather well. The earthen tone was muted and deep, like the red soil near the Draig palace. The sleeves were short, exposing the length of her arms and the skirt fell to her feet. Alek dressed like the others working in the loading dock—loose-fitted pants and a tunic shirt. The lighter colored material made his skin appear darker.

"As soon as the reserve fuel tanks are filled, you can board," Mirek said behind them. They turned to look at the man. "The skies are clear, so takeoff shouldn't be too unsettling." With a small smile, he said to Kendall, "Alek doesn't like takeoffs and landings."

Alek grumbled. "I do fine."

"Fine?" Mirek shook his head in denial. "The first time the ship's safety protocols had to lock you in your seat."

Alek grimaced and lightly rubbed his ass. "I

think I still have the markings from where it suctioned me down."

"No, I didn't see anything," Kendall answered before catching herself. Her mouth dropped open slightly in embarrassment at the unintended admission. Both Mirek and Alek laughed. She felt the heat flaming her cheeks. Luckily, a loud series of metallic clanks drowned out any opportunity to respond and gave her time to regain her composure.

When they could again speak, Alek said, "I was a child when that happened. I still maintain if we were meant to fly our dragons would have wings."

"Don't let him fool you, little sister." Mirek placed his hand on Kendall's shoulder. "There is a reason I don't take this one up into orbit with me very often."

Kendall glanced at her husband in question. He said nothing.

Mirek leaned in to her and loudly whispered, "Just don't sit too close to him."

"All right, enough," Alek said, pushing Mirek's arm to get him to step back. His rueful smile took the sting out of his tone.

"Until we meet again, little sister, many blessings." Mirek bowed. Then, with a meaningful glance at his brother, he backed away toward the entryway. "And the best of luck."

Alek waved his hand in dismissal, turning away from Mirek.

"You two seem very close," Kendall commented.

"We are family."

"Are you going to be all right with flying?" she asked in concern.

"Ignore Mirek. He is having a laugh at my expense."

Metal again clanked, cutting off their conversation. When she could again speak, she said, "So, need me to examine that backside of yours to make sure there's no suction marks?"

Alek smirked, trying to bury his laugh. It didn't work. The sound drew the attention of nearby workers who looked surprised to see the man's amused expression. A few stared longer than they should have. "I'd gladly let you make your own suction marks if you like."

Kendall laughed, not bothering to try to hide her amusement like her husband had. "Looking forward to it."

ALEK PUT on a brave face for his wife, but as the spaceship broke through the atmosphere into deep space, he had to grip the arms of his metal seat to keep from flying out of his chair and taking over the pilot controls to make the ship go back down. His stomach knotted. He was glad he'd decided on a light breakfast. Why did people actually like doing this? Space travel felt too unnatural.

Next to him, Kendall seemed completely at ease. She craned her neck as the metal shield slid down to expose the viewing portal. His home world slowly pulled away from them. Mountains, red with streaks of gray, melded seamlessly with the forest near where his castle home lay nestled in a valley. The path from his home to the palace reminded him of the curve of his wife's hip when she rested on her side. He could almost identify the exact location where he'd kissed her before Aeron's interruption.

The ship changed course, taking the planet out of view. As one of the suns moved past the portal, the transparent material of the screen dimmed to keep the bright light at a safe level for humanoid eyes. Kendall watched until nothing remained in the portal but darkness with dots of starry light.

"I've seen a lot of planets from space," Kendall said, "but your home world is one of the prettier ones. There is no smoke choking your skies and the land is unmarred by metal and glass structures. Some places are so choked up with smog you can't see the ground. Others have buildings over every inch of land."

Alek nodded, forcing himself to relax as the ship stopped bouncing and the ride became smoother.

Kendall slid her hand over his and squeezed. "It was a good takeoff."

Again, he nodded.

"But you're still tense."

He should have known she'd feel his unease. Alek didn't try to deny it.

"You want to show me where our quarters are and I'll help take care of that tension?" She gave him a mischievous smile.

Even with her playful demeanor, he felt the sadness she was trying to hide from him. How did he think he would ever be able to let her go? He'd convinced himself that he'd do the honorable thing, but how could the gods expect him to give up his wife? As the ship flew away from his world, he knew he could never return unless it was as he left —with his bride.

"You seem certain about something." Kendall's smile fell as she studied him. He felt her probing around inside him, trying to make sense of his emotions.

"Only that I wish to get you into my bed. I have

never kissed my wife in space." He lifted her hand to his mouth and kissed it.

As he held her knuckles against his lips, Kendall extended the backs of her fingers against his cheek. "There are several things you've never done to your wife in space." She pushed up from her chair.

The metal walls had a puckered texture that kept them from shining too brightly. The long, arched opening exposed the passageway beyond the wall. Alek began to stand, only to stop as Kendall slid her hand over the wall scanner to close the door.

"These ships have universal lock codes. The pilot can override them..." She pushed at the controls. "...but this will give us privacy unless there is an emergency." The overhead lights dimmed. When she looked at him, a smile curled her lips.

"We don't need locks. None would dare disturb us without permission. It is a perk of our titles."

When he looked at his wife, he felt as if he had run up the side of his planet's steepest mountain. His heart beat faster, his breath quickened, his muscles tensed, all as a euphoric rush invaded his body. He wanted to tell her how he felt, but the words failed him. How did he put into words something so profound, especially when he was not a man used to speaking about his emotions?

Kendall slid onto his lap. Her legs were to the side and her hip nestled next to his waist as she leaned back to run her fingers along his neck. He brought his hand up to support her by the small of her back. With her thumb, she tilted his jaw up. She closed her eyes briefly before whispering, "Mm, I desire you too."

Alek smiled. He did want her, desperately, and she felt it. However, she missed the true depth of his need for her with that statement. Their connection was still new and her oversight was understandable. It wasn't just physical lust, though that was powerful. What he felt was a profoundly emotional necessity. If he'd had his brothers' art for speaking, he would have told her how he felt in perfect detail, but words escaped him. He did the only thing he could—he kissed her.

KENDALL SWALLOWED down her anger and fear to instead focus on her husband's desire. She did not want her last days with Alek to be filled with negativity. The memories she had of him, of his planet, would stay in her mind for a long time. Perhaps he was right. Perhaps there would be a time when she could come back to him. But was it naïve of them to think their feelings would remain unchanged? Her timeline would age her in a way his would not. His lifespan surpassed hers. By the time she came back, she could be an old woman and he would look very close to as he did in this moment. Would it matter if her life as an old woman was extended? Would he want her then?

Out of all the things her father's gambling had done to her, losing Alek was the worst—not the repossession or the constantly broken-down equipment, not even the nights she'd gone without food so Margot had enough rations to eat. The small glimpse of possibilities she saw in Alek's mountain home was more than she'd ever dared to hope for.

Alek moved his lips against hers. His desire grew, pressing against her hip. Confusion warred inside her. She knew what she wanted to do and she knew what she had to do. How could she actually decide such a thing? If she followed her heart and something happened to her father, or to Margot if her father refused to let her take the girl, Kendall would never forgive herself. If she left Alek, her heart would break and she'd never fully recover from it.

Alek tried to pull back. She followed him with her lips, kissing him harder. She blocked her feelings from him, focusing on the desire that always simmered beneath the surface. A desperation filled her, pouring out of her, as her movements became frantic.

Mindlessly, she pulled at his clothing to undress him. She wanted to feel his skin against hers. She needed him like she needed air and food. He was a part of her now. How it had happened she didn't know, but there was no time to question it. They only had a few days.

The tension of takeoff slowly eased from his body as he returned her passion. The familiar comfort of being surrounded by space, of being contained in metal, made her feel safe. There was no wilderness beyond the walls, no hidden monsters in the deep black surrounding them. Any ships would be picked up by sensors. Any intruders would set off security alarms.

She focused completely on her husband—the smell of his skin, the taste of his lips, the feel of his body as he moved beneath her. He tugged at her waist, pulling the skirt of her dress. Their clothes were disheveled as the material clung haphazardly to their bodies. His pants were pulled down just enough to free his arousal. She maneuvered over him, taking him inside her.

They made love slowly, their lips only parting for tiny breaths. A few days on a spaceship was not enough time. How could she be expected to leave him?

Gasping, she drew her head back as her climax washed over her. His body answered hers almost instantly as he stiffened. Alek tightened his arms around her as he pulled her close to him. He pressed his face into her chest.

There was so much she wanted to say, but the words didn't come. Instead, she kissed the top of his head. The heat of his breath hit against her cleavage, uncomfortably warm on her already hot flesh. She didn't care as she stayed in his embrace. Leaning her cheek against his head, she looked out at the darkness of space. The moment would be over before she was ready to leave it.

KENDALL STARED out over the high skies, seeing streaks of color in the distance—magenta and blues smeared over the speckled black. She had lived in space long enough to know the ship was making very good time. She would have wished for engine trouble if not for the fact she wanted to get to Margot.

Except when Alek felt obliged to contact Mirek or speak to the pilot, she stayed with her husband. The Draig crewmen were quiet for the most part, leaving the noble couple alone. The only time she heard them engage in loud conversation was when she wandered close to their common room. They'd been playing some kind of throwing game. When they saw her watching them, they'd quieted and she had taken it as a hint to leave them alone.

While Alek spoke to the pilot, Kendall used the opportunity to send an inquiry to the Exploratory Science Commission about her certification status. She assumed she'd have to restart her classes since there was no telling how much she missed. Hopefully they wouldn't charge her too many late penalties. It had taken a lot of scrimping and saving over the last six years to afford the classes to begin with.

As she waited patiently for the Draig crewman to send her message, she continued to watch the sky. The cockpit was mostly automated. Only one crewman was required to oversee the monitors as they traveled through empty space.

"The transmission is confirmed as received, my lady," the crewman said. "It says to expect a response within three days but it could take up to thirty-one days."

"We'll be at the fueling dock before then," Kendall said, more to herself.

"Yes, my lady." The man confirmed. "I will ensure you receive the response whenever it arrives."

"Thank you." Kendall made a move to leave and stopped. "I wonder, is there any way to access a universal star chart?"

"I will have to search the database, my lady. We were not told to supply such programs on this trip. Anything that was not necessary for our journey has yet to be uploaded. I assure you the ship has passed all safety checks, but we were not expecting to fly and some of the extra conveniences have yet to be installed."

"Does the ESC transmission have a time code embedded in it?" She should be able to understand such a time recording.

The crewman looked. "No, sorry, my lady. It appears to be an automated response from their system."

"Thank you anyway." She reached the door but the man's voice stopped her from leaving.

"We just received an amendment to the message. It says account records that have been inactive for over a star year like the one we're requesting may take longer."

Kendall stiffened. A year? She'd known it was possible she'd been in stasis a long time, but over a year? She vaguely felt herself nodding in the crewman's direction before leaving the cockpit. Numbly, she walked the metal corridors. Her sides began to ache as she thought of the tubes going into Riona's body in the stasis pod.

"Kendall? What is it?" Alek ran toward her, panicked.

"My certification status has been inactive for at least a year," she answered.

"The Fuelologist and Station Engineer certificate? You were able to find out? Can't you reactivate your status?"

"I'm not worried about reactivation. I'm worried that this means I was in stasis for at least a year—wait, no, longer. It would have taken time for them to declare my status inactive. It could have been two years. I've most likely been gone for at least two years. Margot would be fifteen now." Kendall found it hard to breathe. "I have been so focused on getting home to her, I couldn't think of anything else. I should have insisted on finding a conversion chart."

"Kendall, come." Alek tried to lead her from the metal passageway.

"That's not entirely true." She refused to move. "I was too scared to think about what happened to me while I was forced to sleep. I convinced myself it could have only been a few months. No one keeps people in stasis too long. It risks stasis sickness. Why would they risk their cargo like that? I had to be worth something. They took me as payment. I mean…" Kendall panted for air, unable to catch her breath. Her body shook and she couldn't stop the tremors. She gripped her side where the feeding tube would have gone in. "Is that why I kept waking up? To prevent stasis sickness?"

"I don't have the answer for you." Alek touched her arm and she jerked.

"How much did I miss? Margot's birthdays." She rubbed her arms, suddenly cold. "Alek, you don't have young girls on your planet so you can't know what they're like. Thirteen to fifteen are hard years. There are body changes and hormone changes and urges and if there is no one to guide then… Margot isn't prepared to deal with the kind of men who come to the fueling dock, not the kind of men who would notice a pretty young girl. I protected her from those customers. She was never allowed around them. And her schooling and eating and who made sure she dresses properly and what if my father lost the foods stores again, who would ration the portions to make sure they didn't run out? And…and…"

"Kendall, easy," Alek took her arms more forcibly and held tight.

At his touch, her knees weakened and she began to fall. Her heart beat fast and hard. Her lungs felt as if they'd stopped working and she gasped to fill them. Terrible thoughts swam in her brain. So much could happen to an unprotected teenage girl. Margot wasn't prepared. She was rash and had a temper. What if she thought Kendall had abandoned her? Their father wouldn't admit the truth. The child would be alone.

"What if he lost her like he lost me?" Kendall whispered. Tears slid down her face.

"Try to breathe. You are borrowing trouble that may not have happened." He held her upright and pulled her to his chest. "Focus on my voice. Focus on breathing. We will get you to your sister. I promise we will get you to your sister no matter the cost or resources. Whatever has happened, we will find her."

Kendall looked at his mouth, heard his voice but didn't fully process his words of comfort. He lifted her into his arms as she cried and shook. He must have sensed her confusion because he kept repeating himself, promising to help her no matter what it took.

ALEK STARED down at his wife's unmoving body. She'd been so worked up he'd been forced to take her to a medical unit to calm her. It prescribed a sedative, one he felt guilty for giving her considering how long she'd been forced into stasis. He didn't want to, but really he had no idea how to help her. She kept asking him questions, impossible questions, about her sister. He could still see the red marks on her arms where her fingers had begun to scrape at her own skin in her panic.

Considering she'd just discovered she'd lost a

few years of her life, he couldn't blame her for her state. Anger built inside him—anger toward her father, a man who did not deserve Kendall's love. For a man raised with family pride and loyalty, the conclusion was a hard one to admit to. Still, despite her father's lack of worth, Kendall loved the man and Alek had to respect that. His wife's capacity for caring was amazing. That the gods had blessed him with such a woman even more so.

Unwilling to leave her alone in case she awoke, he sat down on the bed next to her and watched her as she slept. His family needed him. With the possible threat of alien invasion coupled with the rumors that had been going around about the Var growing overbold, his family needed him at home more than ever. But how could he leave his wife? How could he leave her to deal with her father alone? He had no clue as to what had happened to her sister.

Alek desperately wished he had answers for her. He wished the problem was before them—visual, fanged and deadly, there to fight. He would tear apart a thousand beasts with his bare hands to protect her. But how did he fight the unknown? How did he protect her from feeling? From pain? From heartache?

He pressed his hand hard against his chest.

Even in sleep her heart ached. He felt it. The emotional pain made it hard for him to breathe. How could anyone do this to such a perfect woman?

Alek balled his hands into fists. He wanted to grab hold of her father and thrash him until he changed his ways and apologized for his sins against his children. If Alek was ever to be blessed with children, he would die rather than hurt them. That was how fathers should be.

"I promise I will do all that is in my power to help you," Alek whispered. He stroked her hair away from her face, watching as the red tips skated over her cheek.

She didn't answer, not that he expected her to. Alek did the only thing he could. He sat in silence for many hours, refusing to leave her side, as he watched over her lest she wake up and need him.

KENDALL MOANED, holding her head. Her movements were sluggish as she tried to concentrate through the fog of her thoughts. Part of her wanted to stay asleep. It would have been easy to just let go and fall back into darkness.

"How are you?" Alek asked, the question pulling her into consciousness.

"Drained," she mumbled. "Or drugged."

"I apologize. I didn't know how else to help you. After all you have been through, I didn't want to force you to sleep, but…" He paused. "I didn't leave your side. You were safe. I give you my word. Nothing happened to you."

She felt his worry and lifted a weak hand to brush against his arm. He sounded as if he'd been practicing his words. "No."

"No?"

Kendall coughed lightly. She closed her eyes and bumped the back of her hand against him in an effort to comfort him. "No, don't apologize. You have been nothing but kind to me."

Warm fingers slid over her wrist, holding her hand against his skin. Her mind drifted and she wasn't sure how much time passed before she opened her eyes again. He still held her arm. His fingers stroked her wrist. Kendall arched her back, stretching as she suppressed a yawn.

"The fueling dock is close."

Kendall blinked, pulling her hand from his grasp as she pushed up on the bed. She suppressed another yawn. "How do you know?"

"The captain made an announcement."

She hadn't heard anything.

"You were sleeping." Alek touched her face.

"What can I get for you? Food? Drink? Change of clothes?"

"Decontaminator," she said. "It might help clear my head."

"Of course." Though his expression was shielded, she knew he worried for her and was sorry for drugging her. She felt him inside her.

"It's all right, Alek." She touched him as he touched her, stroking his cheek. "Feel inside me. I'm all right now. I was under a panic force I couldn't control. Everything rushed in on me. You helped me. I'm not mad. I could never be mad at you. If anything, I'm a little embarrassed by it."

"I have thought about our situation. I can't leave you, Kendall. If you must be here, then I will remain with you."

"But your family? Your home? You have responsibilities."

"My home is with you. You are my wife. I will miss my family, my people, the ceffyls, but you are my wife. Don't ask me to leave you behind. I will give up everything I have just to be near you." His hand shook, the only outward sign of the sacrifice he was making. "My planet is nothing if you are not on it. I thought I could find a way to get you to come back with me, but how can I ask you to leave your sister, your home, for mine? I see, I *feel*, how deeply you care for your life here. How could I expect you to leave it for me when I was not willing to leave mine for you? It was not fair to expect you to live on one planet when clearly in the stars is where you belong. I see your face when you look out into space. Until the panic about your sister overtook you, you were relaxed on this ship like you have never been on world. You don't look at the walls like something is going to jump through them and attack."

"You would give everything up for me?" Kendall didn't need to ask the question. She felt his answer. His gaze shifted, swirling in brilliant gold, showing her the depths of his soul.

"Everything I am has been yours since that first moment I saw you standing beside the fallen tree, blindly reaching out to me in the darkness." He turned his face into her hand, letting his lips brush over skin. "I will learn to live in space. I cannot learn to live without you."

A tear slid over her cheek onto his hand. She knew what this offer cost him. She saw his love of his homeland. She felt the bond he shared with his brothers. She saw the respect his people had for him and the devotion he had to his people. It was in his honorable actions, in his stubborn pride, hidden in the hand-drawn parchments on his table. Kendall thought of those drawings. The great care he'd taken to depict nature proved how much a part of him the wilderness of Qurilixen was.

"I cannot ask you to make that sacrifice." She pulled his hand from her face and dropped her hand from his. "I know what these words are costing you."

Kendall felt the hot tears streaking down her face. She was a fool. How could she think to leave him? Alek offered her love, unconditional love, and she'd planned to throw it all away for a man who'd lost her at a game of cards, or chips, or dice, or whatever failed hot streak was happening at the time. Why? Because a sense of loyalty told her to respect her father no matter what? Since she could remember she'd been taking care of everything—the fueling dock, Margot, customers, her father.

"I'm so confused. I don't know how to feel."

"You don't know how to feel about me staying?" His entire body stiffened.

"My father. I can't hate him," she whispered. "I want to, but I can't. His gambling brought us together and that is something..." Kendall gave a short laugh. "Perhaps it was the will of your gods. If that is true, and you can't fight fate, then how can I hate him for his hand in my fate? Yet everything I know tells me that people make their own fates and my father wronged me."

"The gods give us options. They do not force

our hand. Your father was not helpless in his decisions, but you can handle how you react. You can forgive him. You can be honorable even when others are not."

Kendall smiled. "You have such a good heart. I don't think you know just how rare of a quality that is in the universe. I can't take you away from your family. Living in the stars can be so cold. I want Margot to experience life on world, the warmth and love that you have is... It's amazing. I don't know what's happened to her since I've been gone these past years, but I want my sister to know something better than the fueling docks. I want something better than the fueling docks. I want a life with you and Margot on Qurilixen. I admit my sacrifice will be less than what you were willing to give up for me. I want to invite my father to come and hope that he will heal of his addiction in a stable home with good influences. If he agrees, I will do my best to keep him in line and I apologize in advance for the trouble he will cause, but if he refuses I will take Margot and leave him behind. If he refuses, I can no longer be my father's keeper."

"Your family is always welcome, my lady. If your father will not act the part he was meant by biological ties to play, then I will claim Margot and she will be treated as if she were born to us. All will accept her as a member of the noble family, just as you are family."

Every nerve ending in her body reached for him. Kendall felt his love wash over her. Fear of what she might find still simmered in the depths of her being, but it was outshone by hope and anticipation. For the first time in her life the future didn't look like an endless chore.

"You smell fine," Alek said.

Kendall laughed at the unexpected compliment. "Thanks?"

"I don't think you need to decontaminate. I think you should stay here." Within seconds, she found herself on her back with her husband artfully over her. His thigh pressed up between her legs. He kissed her neck. "I love you, wife. Everything I have is yours."

"I love you, but more than that I appreciate you." She pulled his face to hers and kissed him slowly and passionately. The golden haze of a shift swirled in his eyes. They made love, not needing to speak. The connection between them grew so strong she felt what he wanted without him having to say a word, and she opened herself up fully to him. He entered her when her body was peaked and ready without having to test her depths first. She felt his heart beating and her own resetting it's rhythm to match. When she breathed, she took his air into her lungs. The sensation was unlike anything she'd ever experienced.

Her lids fell heavily over her eyes as pleasure rippled through her. They climaxed in perfect unison. Nothing stood between them. This is what she wanted. Soon, she would have Margot and her life would be perfect.

"I WONDER what Margot looks like. She's probably so pretty. Her mother was beautiful." Kendall could hardly contain herself. Alek glanced down to where she gripped his arm, holding tight. They stood in the cockpit watching as the captain drove the ship to park away from the fueling queue. The ship didn't need to purchase fuel. It was one thing Qurilixen had plenty of.

Alek kept his expression blank, not judging his wife's home. The metal docking lot looked worn, with large dents in the once-smooth metal. The black scorch marks from laser blasts marred the outside surface. "Was there a battle here?"

"Drunken customer. We asked him to leave and he blasted a few shots in protest. We had to send a rescue team out after him a few days later because he'd forgotten to put his ship in the fueling queue when he landed." She glanced up at him and he was lost in her eyes. "This is just as I remember it."

He thought that she might change her mind and decide to stay. If she did, he would stay with her. He had not lied when he told her his life was with her—no matter where that was.

"Loading plank down." The captain said before beginning the long process of powering down the ship. "Feel free to disembark." He proceeded to give commands to his crew to secure the ship and perform safety checks.

"Come. I want to show it to you." Kendall pulled on his arm, leading him to her home. The docking platform was loud and chaotic. Strange smells and even stranger sounds filled the metal space. The workers looked like they hadn't bathed in days and they reeked of fuel. There was no nature, no freshness, and Alek had to concentrate not to breathe too deeply.

An alien with tentacles drifting like strange arms around his head was locking the ship to the deck when they moved to the main walkway. He gurgled noises at Kendall and she lifted her hands, slamming the back of one into the palm of the other. The creature gurgled louder. When a tentacle touched the lock, a suction sound popped over the large docking bay.

The markings along the exit door were universal signs for toilets, decontaminator laser baths, food and lodging. A thin, pale creature pulled a piece of metal from against the wall, causing a flurry of space bugs and rodents out of their hiding spot. Kendall gasped, jumping slightly.

"Who canceled the exterminator? That is not acceptable!" Her tone hardened. She pointed at a nearby worker. "Tell Hark to get the exterminator down here."

The man looked at her, confused. "Hark?"

Kendall stiffened, as if catching herself. "Never mind." Then, under her breath, she said, "I'll do it myself."

As they ventured out of the loading dock to the inner corridors, he watched as tension slowly came over his wife's body. Her gait became longer and her stride more purposeful. She walked easily through the halls, clearly knowing her way through them.

Turning a corner, they met with an information desk. The woman behind it looked to be well at the end of a rougher youth. Tiny lines filtered out from her bored eyes. She glanced up with disinterest as Kendall approached the desk. "I'm seeking Haven. Where is he? Someone blocked the main hall to the offices."

The woman had been sitting staring at her feet,

yet she still managed to look as if Kendall's presence was interrupting her important work.

"Haven," Kendall repeated. She started to place her hands on the dirty metal desk but thought better of it at the last moment and pulled them back.

"Fifty space credits," the woman said.

"I'm not going to pay you," Kendall answered in affront.

"Good luck with the haven thing, organ-beat. We're not into charity." The woman turned her attention back to her feet.

"Fine. I'll go myself the back way."

"Fifty space credits," the woman repeated.

"Show us first and then I'll pay you."

The woman's dark eyes stared for a long moment. Finally, she sighed. "This way," she muttered.

Lack of exercise gave their rude hostess an abundance of curves, not necessarily unflattering but for the ill-fitted cut of her tight clothing. The woman walked as if she had nowhere to be and yet did not want to be where she was. She absently kicked trash from the middle of the hall to the edges. Kendall made small noises of displeasure with each step.

"Cheapest we got. Fifty a night." The woman manually pushed open a metal door and stepped aside. It squeaked on its hinges only to stick before fully opening.

Alek peered into the room. It was a small square, no bigger than a dungeon and not nearly as clean. Black grates covered the walls with hooks for hanging clothing. The lights flickered and buzzed. Holes had been beat into the walls only to be filled with bits of torn material and trash for privacy but it did nothing to block the music coming from a room next door. A woven mat was the only furniture.

"I don't want—" Kendall began.

"I told you, no charity," the woman interrupted. She squashed a bug as it crawled from the room. "You want sanctuary, you have to pay for the privacy like everyone else."

"Not sanctuary, Haven," Kendall corrected.

"I have no idea what you're talking about." The woman sighed. She made a move to leave them. "If you try to stay without paying security will launch you into space without a ship."

Alek placed his hand on his wife's shoulder when she looked as if she might lunge at the hostess.

Kendall glanced in his direction but didn't meet his eyes. He detected her deep embarrassment.

"The owner. Let me talk to the owner," she said.

"That would be my father, but he won't give you a free stay either."

Suddenly, Kendall weakened her stance and wobbled on her feet. Whispering, she breathed more than spoke, "Margot?"

"What?" The woman jerked as Kendall tried to touch her. "I don't have time for this. Owner's down the hall, left, right, left, left, if you get lost bother someone else."

"What happened to you? Don't you remember me?" Kendall asked. "You look nothing like I remember. You're so old."

"Hey!" the woman yelled, finally showing a little bit of passion in her bored existence. "I don't know you, lady, and I sure as piss am not going to listen to your insults. One more word and I'll launch your ass into space myself. "

"I didn't mean. I didn't expect you to be..." Kendall tried to reach out her hand. "I remembered you much younger."

"I warned you!" The woman slapped Kendall's hand back and took off down the corridor at a fast clip. "I need security. Roger!"

"Maybe we should find your father first. Then we will explain things to your sister."

"She didn't recognize me," Kendall said, dazed. "I didn't recognize her."

"It appears as if many years have passed, more

than you thought. At least you know she's alive. Let's find your father before we're asked to leave the dock, then we can proceed with how to handle Margot." Alek led her away from the screaming hostess in the direction of the offices.

Kendall stumbled. "It's too late to help her. What has happened to this place? It was never this dirty. Margot, she had to be, what? Thirty? Forty? That means I was in stasis for…"

Alek lifted his wife into his arms as she began to tear up. She clung to him. He strode down the hall, aware of the security calls echoing behind them.

"They stole my life," she said into his neck.

"You have a new life," Alek answered. Her grief rolled over him, tainted with her disappointment. She'd been so eager to find her sister, to raise her like the daughter she, by all rights, was. The bored creature they found was not the Margot of Kendall's memory.

Kendall pushed weakly at Alek. "Here. Set me down. I'll be all right."

He stopped and obeyed. Kendall held on to his arm as she righted herself. Then, turning, she marched down the corridor and up a narrow row of stairs with renewed purpose born of anger.

KENDALL REFUSED to succumb to another force of panic. Though dirtier than she'd left it, she still knew her way through the station. At the top of the stairs, she glanced into her office as she passed, noting the stacks of liquor crates where her desk had been. In her mind only a few months had passed. In reality, it had been a lifetime. Her natural timeline had been delayed, her past erased while she slept.

"Father!" Kendall yelled as she whipped around the door frame to her father's office. "I'm home!"

Her heart hammered in her chest. The room was changed, not that she was surprised. It took her eyes a moment to adjust before she found the man she sought sitting at a desk. He was hunched over, his back toward them.

"Surprise," she announced angrily. Feeling Alek behind her gave her strength, but at the same time it helped her to control her rage. If he had not been here, supporting her, she might have attacked.

The man turned a little too quickly at the intrusion. He blinked heavily as he set down a glass of liquor. Red-rimmed eyes stared drunkenly at her. "Wh-what?"

Kendall couldn't move, couldn't speak. Her mouth opened but words would not leave her.

"Haven," Alek said. "I am Lord Aleksej,

Younger Duke of Draig, husband to your daughter."

"Husband? Beatrice married?" The man swayed in his seat.

"Alek, no," Kendall managed. "He's not my father."

"Wait. You're looking for Haven?" The drunkard put forth. "You're about five years too late. I'm Cinder. This is my dock."

"He lost the docks, didn't he?" Kendall concluded. Part of her was relieved that the rude hostess wasn't Margot. In light of what she'd thought moments before, five years wasn't as bad as thirty.

"You're one of his daughters? I heard he sold you all to Kintok slavers, but then you wouldn't be here...at least not in one piece." He seemed to sober some. "Guess that was just a rumor. I also heard he lost you girls at cards, or that you died and he buried you in the walls. It would seem that the card story is more likely. This the guy who won you?"

Kendall didn't satisfy the man's curiosity with an answer. "Do you know where I can find him?"

"Sorry, like I said, you're about five years too late. All I know is the guy lost everything. I bought this place off a Larceny Casino auction. The way I heard it, when they came to take the docks his heart gave out. There wasn't much left that he didn't lose gaming. The casino collected most of it in pieces. The place was a wreck when I got here. " Cinder turned and began rummaging through his desk.

Kendall glanced toward the dirty hall and said under her breath, "Yeah, you really fixed the place up nice."

Alek arched a brow. Kendall frowned.

"Thank you," Cinder answered, not catching the sarcasm in her tone. "I have to warn you, if you're looking for an inheritance, there isn't anything. The casino gave me some paperwork in case any relatives stopped by and tried to make a claim. I have all the documentation around here somewhere. From what I could tell, his most valuable property besides the docks were a couple ships called *The Margot* and *The Can-something*."

"Kendall?" Kendall asked.

"Yeah, that's it. *The Kendall.* They're long gone. The casino took those before I got here. There were some old files, clothes, but they all came with the deal so I had every legal right to sell them."

"I'm not looking to rob you," Kendall said in irritation. She pointed at his deck when Cinder stopped looking. "The paperwork. Does it say who bought *The Margot*?"

The man pulled out an electronic clipboard. Its

surface was scratched and dusty. "I don't know. Truth is there was no money to be made in someone else's lost property, so I didn't bother to read it all."

Kendall crossed his office and took the clipboard from him. Her hands shook. "I'm taking this." She didn't give him a choice. "My husband will give you contact information." She glanced at Alek who nodded in agreement. "If anyone else comes looking, you have them find me."

Alek went to the desk and she heard him dictating instructions to the man. Kendall slid her finger over the clipboard. The screen lit up and automatically started playing an advertisement for the casino. She numbly watched smiling, happy faces as person after person was shown scoring it big. It was all faked and it made her sick to her stomach. After the ad finished a menu appeared with the documentation she sought.

"Come on, Kendall. Let's go back to the ship and look at this data. Cinder has agreed to call off his daughter's security." Alek placed his hand on the small of her back and ushered her through the office door. The sound of drinking followed them out. Cinder belched, clearly resuming his efforts to find oblivion. "Unless there is someone you would like to see first?"

"I only recognized a few of the workers," she

said absently, staring at the electronic clipboard. "The casino listed us as ships. That's why they kept me in stasis so long. They had to hide the fact they took a person and make sure no one protested." As they passed her old office, she suddenly stopped. Holding the clipboard to Alek, she said, "Hold this, please. I have to check something."

Kendall glanced around to make sure they weren't being watched before slipping into the office turned liquor storage. It was tight around the crates and her shirt snagged on a piece of splintered wood. One of the crates had been opened and the bottles matched those littering Cinder's office.

Leaning over, she ran her hand over the wall. The dark made it hard to see, but she didn't need light to find what she was looking for. Her finger fit against a small groove. A tiny green glow appeared as a sensor scanned her fingerprint. Seconds later, a small door in the wall opened. Reaching inside, she pulled out a tiny leather pouch.

Pressing the secret compartment shut, she joined Alek in the hall. At his quizzical look she lifted the small treasure. "Right where I left it."

"What?" Beatrice's yell sounded from behind them. "I want her gone. She's nothing but..." The hostess saw them and pointed a finger in their direction. "You're out of here. Get your ship and take off."

Kendall fisted her hand over the pouch. "Quit your yelling. We got what we came for." That wasn't exactly true. "After I secure this on the ship, I want to walk around before we leave," she said to Alek. "Maybe someone will know more about my sister. Maybe someone who worked for us is still here."

"Of course," he agreed.

Kendall lifted up on her toes and kissed him. "Thank you."

She led the way back to the docking lot in silence. Once back on the ship, she stashed the pouch and the clipboard in their room. They discovered from the captain, who Alek ordered to prepare for takeoff, that the Draig crew had left to explore and find local food.

"The diner," Kendall said, leading the way from the dock back into the main complex. Indeed, the men were in the small diner. The only thing Kendall could say about the place she'd eaten more meals than she cared to remember was that at least it was clean. Seeing a short, round gelatinous woman, Kendall rushed forward. "Vanni. It's you, isn't it?"

"Mistress Kendall?" The waitress paused before setting down two squirming plates of bugs. Her light-blue dress hugged tight to her frame. The material contrasted her green skin and accented her blue hair. Her voice had a husky quality to it, more so than Kendall remembered. "You haven't aged an hour. I never took you for one of those enhancement types. Though what do I know? I suppose not all humans age like the rest of us."

"I was locked in stasis." Kendall hugged the woman. Her arms sunk into the gelatinous form before she let go. "And I never took you for the shrinking type. You haven't been taking care of yourself."

"Stasis preservation?" Vanni eyed Alek before turning her attention back to the girl. "You left so suddenly. I didn't think you'd ever come back here. Not sure why you would."

"I was repossessed, but I'm fine."

"Lost in a wager, I know. It took us a while to figure out what happened to you, but your father let it slip once to some of the dock hands. I'm glad to see you survived whatever it was he sold you into." She again looked at Alek.

"Vanni, this is my husband, Alek."

"Greetings," Alek said.

Vanni nodded in acknowledgement but didn't speak to him. "I'm glad to see you are well, but what are you doing back here? There's nothing here for you. Almost everyone left after you disappeared. Things fell apart. Wages weren't paid. Then after Margot, well, now there's only myself and Ger out on the docks. Still can't understand a blasted thing the man says."

"What happened to Margot?"

"She got into a lot of fights after you left. We looked after her the best we could, but then a few years after you left a couple of men came and took her. After that your father lost just about anything that wasn't soldered down."

"Do you know who took her? Where?"

"Sorry, I don't. They had salvage uniforms on. I seem to recall one of the girls overhearing something about a spa service, but I wouldn't bet my life on it. I can only guess they were the same men who took you."

"Is this…*moving*?" One of the Draig crewmen stood, dropping his eating utensil.

Vanni gave a small laugh before hardening her expression. Loudly, she stated, "Elteeb stew. Only thing we serve. Food simulators have been gone since your father lost them."

"Kendall?" Alek touched her shoulder. She turned to bury her face in his chest. Her arms wrapped around his waist, holding him tight.

"I'm going to find out everything I can about Margot from Vanni. She doesn't like men but will talk freely if I'm alone. Please, take the crew back to the ship. I'll be there soon." When it looked like he would protest, she put her hand on his mouth. "I'll be fine. The biggest threat is Beatrice, and I can handle her."

"As you wish, my lady," Alek agreed. He barked an order to the men in his gruff Qurilixen tongue. The men instantly stood and left the diner.

Vanni watched after them before turning expectantly to Kendall. She tilted her head toward an empty table. Kendall nodded, joining the waitress.

KENDALL LEARNED nothing from Vanni other than what she could pretty well guess on her own. Margot had been angry when Kendall left, confused as to why her sister had abandoned her. She'd cried for days, had been ignored by their father, fought with strangers, was accused of stealing and finally was repossessed. Rumors of a spa planet were just that—rumors. Just as they hadn't known where Kendall was, they didn't know where Margot had been taken. None were surprised. Margot was a burden on her father who didn't know the first thing about raising an angry, hormonal teenage girl. After Margot was taken and with no one around to keep him in check, Haven spiraled out of control. He drank too much, ate too much, gambled even more and flew himself head-first into his own grave when he succumbed to heart failure.

Gone, thought Kendall. *My sister is gone.*

"Kendall?" Alek whispered, reaching for her on their bed. They had watched the fueling dock disappear as the captain flew the ship back to Qurilixen.

"I didn't say anything," she answered. Her mind raced and she was unable to rest.

"Your thoughts are loud." Alek pulled her body against his, holding her. "I promise I will help you find out what happened to your sister." He paused. "You read the documents twenty times. There is nothing there."

"You're worried about me, and the Tyoe, and Margot and your family," Kendall said. "You can't hide your thoughts from me either."

Kendall felt her husband's desire for her. He wanted her, always wanted her, but tonight he was content to simply hold her close. There was no lack of passion in their marriage, but the true blessing was to have someone who cared for her so deeply and completely.

"My father is dead," she said. There was no point in keeping silent as they were both awake. "I can believe it, but at the same time I wasn't prepared for it. It's strange. I thought I'd be riddled with grief, and I am sad, but at the same time…"

"There is no shame if you feel a sense of relief. Your father was a troubled man. I can't imagine he would lose both his daughters gambling and remain unaffected." Alek pulled her closer. He settled his hand over hers. The small stone of her mother's ring pressed into his palm. It is what she'd taken from the pouch—the only thing that had been left on the fueling dock that could be called hers. "There was nothing you could do for him."

"I was asleep when they took Margot. I guess it doesn't matter how fast I got there. I wouldn't have been able to save her." Kendall sniffed as a tear rolled over her cheek. "I have to find her, Alek. I have to do something, but I don't know where to look."

"Let me think about it and I will come up with a plan." He kissed her head. "We will not stop until we find out what happened to your sister."

ALEK DIDN'T SLEEP as he watched over his wife. She drifted in and out of consciousness. Her pain was his and he wished nothing more than to take all of it from her and into himself. That is how he spent his nights. His days were by her side making sure she ate, doing his best to distract her mind and listening when he could not.

Conditions made flying hard and their return trip was delayed by over a week. Solar flares emitting a high-energy radiation from several directs forced the ship to pause. Apparently, these occurrences were rare, but to fly through them proved to be dangerous to human DNA. With Kendall onboard, they weren't taking chances. By the time Qurilixen showed itself on the viewing screen, he had yet to sleep for longer than an hour at a time.

"Home," Kendall whispered as the ship touched down. The loud hiss of the ship's engines echoing off the stone walls was only outdone by the scrap of the overhead camouflage sliding back into place to hide the ship within the mountain. They stayed strapped into their seats until the vibrations stopped, indicating the engines were off.

Alek slipped his arm around his wife's shoulders as they disembarked. She returned his embrace, giving him a small smile as she curled her fingers over his waist. The sadness was there within her, but so was her love. He longed for the day he'd be able to feel the sadness fade.

"This is how you obey orders?" Bron said, his tone even.

Alek grimaced. Bron waited by the closed door with Mirek.

"Are we in trouble?" Kendall whispered.

"I will handle it," Alek assured her.

"You should have not pulled rank like a pouting child," Mirek said in their shared tongue. "Be happy Alek brings home his bride. You ordered the marriage settled. It's settled. I sent guards to the forest to watch for the Tyoe and your wife is dealing with the communication system."

Kendall glanced up at Alek, not understanding Mirek's words.

"Well-kept secret, brother," Alek grumbled to Mirek, slipping easily into the Qurilixian language.

"He sent someone to the cabin to check on you," Mirek answered. "I had no choice."

"I thought the Tyoe kidnapped you." Bron frowned. "You should have told me you had urgent business off world."

"Don't be dramatic," Mirek interrupted. "It did not get that far. I told you before you had time to send out search parties."

"You would have forbidden me from taking her back." Alek hadn't known when he left if Kendall would be returning with him. Bron would have ordered all the ships grounded in an effort to save Alek's marriage.

"Yes," Bron agreed. "I am glad you are home safe. Is all taken care of?"

"Later," Alek said, not wanting to talk about it in front of his wife. Even if Kendall couldn't understand what they were saying, he didn't want to keep excluding her from the conversation. He switched to the star language. "Asking me to fix the communication devices was like asking me to fly this ship. I couldn't find the control panel."

"You are lucky my wife knows more about communications than anyone on this planet. She's agreed to oversee repairs." Bron gave a slight smile. "So you don't have to worry about it."

"Any word on the Tyoe?" Kendall asked. "Are we safe?"

"Don't worry, little sister, we will protect you." Bron reached his hand out and touched her shoulder briefly.

Mirek opened the door and led the way into the corridor. "We can find no immediate threat. As soon as the pilot is rested, I will check out things from space. I will ensure the planet is safe and I will send inquiries to friends. I sent a few runners to try to bring some of the other pilots back, but they're hunting and can't be found. I don't expect them back for some time. We will learn everything there is to discover about the Tyoe. If there is to be a battle, we will be ready."

"Has Lady Riona awakened?" Alek asked.

Mirek inhaled a deep breath and held it.

"No," Bron answered for him. He stepped behind his brother as they made their way single file down a long flight of stairs. The halls were narrower in this part of the home. "But we take care of our own."

Kendall pulled on Alek's arm, stopping him. When the brothers had made their way several steps ahead, she asked softly, "Should I tell him how long I was in stasis? It might help to know that after five or so years I am relatively healthy. Riona should be all right as far as the stasis goes if I am any example."

"Yes, sister, it helps," Mirek answered.

Kendall stiffened. "I have to get used to the hearing thing," she said under her breath.

Alek kissed her softly. She was so precious to him, and so adorable in her embarrassment. "Let me take you to our home so you can settle after the flight. I have a few things to discuss with my brothers before I join you."

"Yes, but don't take too long. Hopefully you can sleep now that we are on land. I don't like you sitting up for days at a time. It can't be good for your mind."

"You question my sanity?" He arched a brow.

"Never." She kissed him back, slid her tongue into his mouth and moaned softly into him.

When she pulled away, he announced to his brothers, "Don't expect me until tomorrow. Bron, you can yell at me then."

His brothers chuckled, not stopping their progress down the stairs.

"I THOUGHT you were going to be unavailable until tomorrow." Mirek looked up from the viewing table and scratched his head as he arched his back in a long stretch.

Alek recognized the star charts as their sky. "What are those red markings?"

"Radiation signatures." Mirek suppressed a yawn. "I'll get better readings from the sky. If anyone was in our space, they should have left a trail. Honestly though, all these signatures are old. I'm not sure we'll find many answers here."

"When you're up there, I need you to try to reach Lochlann," Alek said. Long-distance communications worked better from space than on land. The messages were routed through stations until they were picked up by the right vessel.

Mirek's hand dropped from his head to the table. "That traitor? You think he has something to do with the Tyoe?"

"No. It's for Kendall." Alek explained what happened to the two sisters. Mirek frowned, not meeting his eyes.

"I only tell you because Kendall gave me

permission. She is anxious to see her sister come home. I've tried to think of another way, but Lochlann is the only one I know who travels the more questionable circles of space."

Lochlann was a childhood friend and one who was currently flying the high skies with a Var shifter, and not just any Var shifter, but Prince Jarek of the Var. To say his name often incited feelings of disappointment and anger between the brothers.

"Of course we must find Margot. She is family." Mirek nodded. It didn't matter that he'd never met the girl. "But Lochlann? He left us."

"I know." Alek nodded.

"With a Var prince," Mirek insisted.

"I know."

"A *pirate* Var prince."

"I know!" Alek slashed his hand. "I don't like what Lochlann did, flying off like that, but he's the only one we can ask. There has to be some Draig loyalty left in the man. I promised Kendall we'd do everything we could to find her sister. It is either Lochlann or I take my wife to space to look for the girl."

"You in space?" Mirek quirked a brow.

"For Kendall, yes, me in space."

"I don't like this idea, but I'll do it. You wouldn't know the first thing about dealing with aliens to get information. Not all of them succumb to torture." Mirek glanced to where his wife lay in stasis. "If it was for my wife, I would say yes. I can't deny helping yours."

"Thank you." Alek clenched his teeth. Lochlann was the last person he wanted to ask for a favor.

"He once asked if he could return to his position in the army," Mirek said. "Bron refused. The war was over and Lochlann's leaving too new. I'll see if he's still interested in coming home. If he finds the girl, I'll let him know that it will go a long way into earning our forgiveness."

"That is why you're the diplomat. You can sell anything." Alek went to Mirek's liquor storage and took out a bottle. "You're running low on stock. You're drinking too much."

"Coming from the man I confiscated nef from." Mirek pressed a few buttons, clearing the viewing table. "What about the casino? Something should be done. They should not be able to treat people like cargo."

"If we fight them, they will never tell us what we need to know. If there is a trace of Margot, they would destroy it before we had a chance to find it. As much as I hate it, there is nothing we can do to them at the moment. But, as soon as we have Margot, we will figure out something." Alek poured a couple glasses and set one down in front of him.

"I am glad your marriage is settled. I see it in your wife's face when she looks at you. I only hope to one day be so blessed."

"You are blessed," Alek said. "Your wife will awaken when it is time for her to do so. The gods have their reasons."

"You say that now, but last time you were in this room you would not have been so confident." Mirek drank the contents down in one gulp. "Go back to your wife and find sleep. You look like something that came out of the backend of a yorkin."

KENDALL STRETCHED her arms over her head, feeling Alek approach before she saw him come up the stairs. Without getting out of bed, she reached out to him. "There you are. I wondered how long you were going to be gone."

"I thought you would still be sleeping." He pulled his shirt over his head and tossed it aside.

"I couldn't sleep without you." She let her arms drop and settled for watching him disrobe. A soft light caressed his muscular body.

"I spoke to my brother." Alek told her of the plan to find Margot. It wasn't much, but it was a start. "After Mirek's, I stopped to check with Cenek about the ceffyls."

"Everything all right?"

"Yes. We confirmed another one is pregnant. It's a good omen this late in the season, and the late season births statistically go well. The elders take it to mean this will be a fertile year for our people." He gave her a meaningful look.

Kendall quirked a brow. "Fertile year? Should I be worried?"

"Do you want children?"

"Right now all I want is you." She smiled at him. "If children come, they come."

He pushed his pants from his hips and crossed the room to join her on the bed. Pulling her into his arms, he held her close. After a long kiss, he whispered, "Do you think you can be happy here on one planet? I know it's not the fueling dock, or a constant parade of new alien creatures, but I promise to do everything I can to make you happy."

"I've been thinking about that." She stroked his face. "I want to finish my Exploratory Science Commission certificate. I think I can be of some use to the mining operation. With a couple extra classes I should be able to switch part of my studies from Station Engineer to Mining Engineer. I can even do my final experiments on *galaxa-promethium*."

Just talking about it excited her. She pushed up on the bed. "Usually the samples are so expensive, and from what I gather there are just layers and layers of it beneath Qurilixen's surface. Do you think you can take me to see the mines?"

"Yes, you can tour the mines, get whatever certificate you like and play with as many rocks as pleases you." Alek pulled her back down onto the bed. "You know, wife, another man might get jealous to see his woman get that excited about rocks."

"Well then, husband. What are you offering that's more exciting than the isotopic properties of *galaxa-promethium*? I have to warn you. I really do like my minerals."

With that, he pushed up from the bed. She frowned as he left her and disappeared into a small doorway in the corner of the room. "Alek? Where are you going? I was joking. I don't like minerals more than you. Alek?"

He reemerged carrying a small box. He crawled onto the bed and knelt beside her and handed her the container. Kendall held the fur coverlet to her chest as she sat up. Slowly, she opened the container. Tiny blue and white gems cut into the shape of stars glistened in the dim light. She lifted the delicate necklace.

"Since you do not live amongst the stars

anymore, I thought it only right that I bring the stars to you so you may carry them with you always."

"Where did you get this?" she asked. No one had ever given her such an expensive gift. "These are starstones. They're even rarer than *galaxa-promethium*."

At that, he chuckled. "Only you would compare jewels to ore. When you were talking to Vanni, I traded for them. You were willing to give up a life up there for one down here. I wanted you to have a piece of the heavens to keep with you."

Kendall gently put the necklace back in its container and set it on the floor next to the bed. This time when she settled into his arms it was to kiss him, and she didn't intend to ever let him go.

"I love you, stubborn, perfect man," she whispered against his mouth.

"And I you, my lady, forever."

EPILOGUE

"Oh, but we found…" Kendall stopped herself. She looked guiltily at her new brothers and then at Alek. He sat next to her on Mirek's couch, his arm tucked around her waist. It was a little uncomfortable on her lower back, but she liked being held by him so didn't say anything. The second she thought it, Alek shifted his arm up and settled it on her shoulders.

"What?" Bron and Mirek demanded at the same time.

"I win the treasure hunt." Alek grinned.

"You mean?" Bron asked in surprise. "Great-grandfather's liquor stash?

"What do you mean *we* found?" Alek said to Kendall. "You stared at me like I had lost my mind."

"You were the one rubbing yourself against the wall." Kendall laughed.

"Where was it?" Bron insisted. "Which wall?"

"The legend was right too. There is a very fine bottle of Qurilixian rum and several Var vintages." Alek pulled Kendall closer to his side.

"Where is it?" Bron demanded louder.

"So you can help yourselves?" Alek chuckled. "No. I won. It's my treasure. Future generations will be trying to find old Draig Alek's stash someday."

"Yes, future generations." Bron smiled. It was a small gesture at first but then it grew wider and uncontained.

"Bron, are...?" Alek began. "Are you saying...?

"Thank you, Mirek. She looks comfortable." Aeron appeared from inside the newest addition to Mirek's home. The stasis room was much bigger than the box Riona had been sleeping in. At the others' attention, she stopped. "Why are you all staring at me like that?"

"She is," Alek said. "I should have seen it earlier."

"Seen what?" Mirek asked, clueless.

"Aeron's pregnant," Alek announced. "Can't you see the glow?"

"We're not all ceffyl breeders, Alek. It's not like

we can see some magical force telling us when a woman is pregnant," Mirek said.

"Did you just call me a ceffyl?" Aeron gasped.

"What?" Mirek shot up from his seat. His guilt over the helpless situation with his wife often caused him to treat Aeron a little more delicately. "I didn't mean... You're not a ceffyl. You're very beautiful."

"Easy," Bron stated. "She's teasing you."

Mirek relaxed back into his seat but still watched Aeron for any signs of displeasure.

"I am teasing," Aeron assured him, "and I am very much pregnant."

The room exploded with congratulations. But just as suddenly the mood fell as Aeron turned to where her sister lay frozen in time. "I only wish Riona was awake to share this moment with me."

"Her skin is looking better," Kendall offered. "That has to be a good sign. The doctors did say that she would probably wake up on her own."

"She does look better," Aeron agreed. She softly touched her stomach. They sat in silence for a long moment. Then Aeron turned her attention back to them. "What is this about a treasure?"

"Our great grandfather hid some of the best liquors known to Draig somewhere in this castle and Alek claims to have found it," Bron said.

"I did find it," Alek asserted, not bothering to

tell his brothers the treasure wasn't in the castle home but rather at the cabin.

"He did," Kendall affirmed. She ran her hand over his thigh, letting the tips of her fingers lightly dance along the muscle.

"I think he should prove it." Bron reached his hand to his wife, urging her next to him on the couch.

"I'll prove it when Riona is awake and all of us brothers and our wives can be together. Until then, it will remain untouched." Alek kissed Kendall's head, leaving his face turned into her hair. She felt the heat of his breath against her scalp.

"Unpregnant wives," Aeron corrected. "I can't drink until after the baby is born."

"Unpregnant wives," Alek amended.

"Hopefully that won't be any time soon." Without caring who watched, Bron leaned over, kissed her stomach and murmured to his unborn child in the gruff Qurilixian language before adding in the star language, "I want many children and plan to keep your mother pregnant for a long time."

Aeron arched a brow at her husband's plan but said nothing. Kendall watched Mirek and Alek, but they didn't seem to think Bron's behavior odd.

Aeron stroked her husband's head. "He already talks to my stomach more than me."

"That's not true," Bron said to her waist. "I'm talking to both of you."

"Come," Alek whispered, his face nuzzling around to her ear and neck. "I should like to see you pregnant."

Kendall gave a short laugh. Seeing Aeron's eyes on her, she shrugged. "They're nothing if not subtle."

Alek persisted, easily convincing Kendall to follow him home. She was beginning to learn her way through the halls, but tonight couldn't concentrate long enough to navigate. Instead, she followed her husband's quick steps as he practically raced to get her alone.

In the back of her mind she thought of her sister. The Draig warrior Alek had sent after Margot was an expert in space navigation and politics. There had been no real news yet, but already the man had reported several leads.

Mirek's expedition into space had been most telling. There were signatures of another spacecraft in their area, both in the sky and in the mountains, but no ship to connect it to. Whoever had kidnapped Bron had left their airspace. The brothers were convinced the Tyoe planned something. Precautions were being taken to ensure the family's protection.

"Try not to worry," Alek said. "The gods

brought you to me for a reason. We have to be fated. You were in stasis for five years. I had to go to five ceremonies before finding you. See, proof that I was waiting for you to come to me."

Kendall still wasn't sure she believed in his gods, but she found comfort in his certainty. Maybe there was something to it. How else could she explain being brought to Qurilixen out of all the planets in the known universes, finding not only a wonderful home but a husband she loved more than herself? For now, all that could be done was being done. Perhaps the gods would find a way to bring Margot to her. If that happened, then she would believe.

As he pulled her into their home, Alek swept her into his arms. All thoughts and worry died in his kiss, leaving only the warmth of their love.

The E...wait a minute.

CHAPTER 17
WAIT A MINUTE, WHAT ABOUT MARGOT?!

I'm sure a lot of you are wondering about Margot (and possibly poised to send me emails demanding answers—send away, I love hearing from you, but don't expect me to give away the details). Right now, you know as much as Kendall does. Don't despair. Her story is coming. Watch for her in a future *Space Lords* series book "His Metal Maiden" where all your Margot Haven questions will be answered.

I know several of you are new to the Dragon Lords, and some have been following them since that first book published in 2004. To each of you, thank you. I often get asked about the future of the series installments. Currently, there are several series installments (each with several books released/planned): Dragon Lords, *Lords of the Var*®,

Space Lords, Zhang Dynasty, Galaxy Playmates (short stories). Beyond these I have even more spin off series planned. Be sure to visit my website often where you can find a complete up-to-date reading order list for all of the futuristic series.

As always, I love hearing from readers. You can email me through my website and let me know which books you want more of...just don't expect me to tell you what happens next.

Michelle M. Pillow
www.michellepillow.com

The End

The Series Continues with
Dragon Lords: The Reluctant Lord

Read *Space Lords: His Metal Maiden*
to find out about Margot.

THE SERIES CONTINUES...

Need more Dragon Lords?
The books continue!
Dragon Lords 7: The Reluctant Lord

Want to see how King Attor's sons turn out,
despite their father's teachings?
Lords of the Var®: The Savage King

Want to see how the King and Queen met?
Dragon Lords 9: The Dragon's Queen

Read all the Dragon Lords and Var books?
Yay, you, keep going!
Space Lords 1: His Frost Maiden

Dragon Lords and *Lords of the Var*® in Modern Day Earth?

Captured by a Dragon-Shifter: Determined Prince

Dragon-shifter Romance
by Michelle M. Pillow

Polished, dignified and reserved in all things. That is a true nobleman.

Lady Clara of the Redding, a living statue of perfection, has been raised a true Redde noblewoman. She has been taught to never show emotion, to never raise her voice, to touch as little as possible, and to never act wildly or rashly. According to her people's custom, the new generation cannot begin until the current one is settled. She is the last of her siblings without a husband and her pregnant sisters will remain in stasis until she's married.

After Clara denies all suitable males on her

home world, her parents are left with one choice— send her to a primitive planet where several noblemen await marriage. The men hardly appear picky about their choices, a perfect arrangement for a reluctant bride.

An uninhibited woman to match his untamed soul. That would be his ideal wife.

Lord Vladan, Ealdorman Honorary of the Draig is not like his noble brothers. Adopted into their family after a mining accident killed his parents, he is every bit as titled as his new brothers, and every bit as welcome into the fold. Yet he can't help but feel the pull of his commoner past. He loves his family, and will always do as duty demands, but a part of him still yearns to shift into dragon form and run free in the wild. It is a side he indulges every chance he gets. This is how he knows his bride will be the most wild of creatures, for he wants passion, not perfection. Surely the gods are mistaken when they bind him to the most refined, reserved, frustratingly *perfect* creature in the universe.

To find out more about Michelle's books visit www.MichellePillow.com

***New York Times* & *USA TODAY*
Bestselling Author**

Michelle loves to travel and try new things, whether it's a paranormal investigation of an old Vaudeville Theatre or climbing Mayan temples in Belize. She believes life is an adventure fueled by copious amounts of coffee.

Newly relocated to the American South, Michelle is involved in various film and documentary projects with her talented director husband. She is mom to a fantastic artist. And she's managed by a dog and cat who make sure she's meeting her deadlines.

For the most part she can be found wearing pajama pants and working in her office. There may or may not be dancing. It's all part of the creative process.

Come say hello! Michelle loves talking with readers on social media!

www.MichellePillow.com

facebook.com/AuthorMichellePillow

twitter.com/michellepillow

instagram.com/michellempillow

bookbub.com/authors/michelle-m-pillow

goodreads.com/Michelle_Pillow

amazon.com/author/michellepillow

youtube.com/michellepillow

pinterest.com/michellepillow

COMPLIMENTARY EXCERPTS

HIS FROST MAIDEN

BY MICHELLE M. PILLOW

Read all the Dragon Lords and Var books?
Yay, you, keep going!

A Qurilixen World Novel
Space Lords Book One by Michelle M. Pillow
Bestselling Futuristic Romance Series

Empath and space pirate, Evan Cormier is obsessed with decoding an ominous premonition about his future. When a fellow crewman angered a spirit, the vengeful Zhang An took her wrath out on everyone in the vicinity. Evan just happened to be one of them. He's now facing a future in which he'll be forever alone.

Lady Josselyn of the House of Craven has been betrayed. With her home world on a Florencian moon under attack and her family dead, she finds herself at the mercy of the one who deceived them. There is only one thing left to do—die with honor. But before she can join her family in the afterlife, she must first avenge all that she held dear. Falling in love with a pirate was never in the plan. Evan and his thieving crewmates might have delayed her fate, but they can't stop destiny.

Frost Maiden Excerpt

Craven Estates, Earth Settlement, Florencia's Fifth Moon

"Lift her," the General ordered, his shiny boots walking away from her, taking her reflection with it.

Two men hauled her to her feet, holding her up by her arms. Josselyn suppressed a cry as they jerked her dislocated shoulder. She couldn't see their faces, didn't need to. Her body hurt so badly she couldn't tell where the pain was coming from anymore.

The one who'd betrayed them stood before her. General Jack Stephans. He'd deceived her family and the fifth moon settlement. He'd traded them in for money and power. Josselyn lifted her gaze briefly to the hard depths of the steel green eyes before her. She wanted to kick, to give one last good blow, to go down fighting, but she couldn't raise her limbs.

"Poor little Josselyn, so heartbreaking," the General grabbed her chin and swiped beneath her eye. He looked young, was in fact very young for his position, only a few years older than her six and twenty. And yet they all knew so much more of fighting than anyone their age should, than anyone ever should.

"We gave you a home," she whispered. "How could you do this? How could you join them?"

"You gave me a place in your stables," he spat, his grip tightening on her chin, bruisingly so. "Not a place at your table. Not a place by your side. Not equal. They gave me a rank, a title. They give me respect. They give me a place in this world."

"Jack," she said, her voice softening for the orphan boy they'd found over twenty years ago. If she begged him, maybe fate could be turned around; maybe this day could be erased. Fate had spit them out in a whirlwind of chance and deceit. Maybe all that had happened wasn't his fault. Maybe it wasn't hers. None of it mattered. None of it changed the fact that he had taken everything she held dear, everyone, and now he was robbing her of her family home. Her tone hardened and she closed her eyes. "General."

"Look at me, Josselyn," he said. His tone

caught even as his grip on her face tightened until his fingers pressed the inside of her cheeks against her teeth. "You're so cold. Even now, your face is composed. Is one, lonely tear all the passion you can muster?"

"I am Lady Josselyn of the House of Craven." Her eyes opened slowly, focusing on the shiny white of his uniform. It gleamed with the orange glow coming from the fireplace. The material looked odd in the drabber earth tones many on the fifth moon wore. Theirs was a world based on Medieval Earth. Each moon in the Florencian system was different, each settlement patterned off a singular time in the human past, times that history had almost forgotten. But the principals of the ancestors who'd established the colonies no longer applied. Times were different now. What had started as preservation of history had turned into reality, into laws and a way of life they all believed in as generation after generation was raised into the worlds of the Florencian moons.

The General shook her by the face until finally she forced her eyes to meet his. He looked angry, hurt, wildly hopeful. "I can save you. I can say you had nothing to do with the treachery of your family. No one wants to kill a woman of noble blood. The line of Craven doesn't have to die. I will take your name; the name denied me by your father."

Was he serious? She knew he'd asked her father for her hand in marriage. In fact, she'd dismissed the proposal with the full knowledge he only asked because he wanted power. Did he think she could love him now? Want him? Take him into her bed?

He must have read the answer on her face because his own expression hardened. She knew Jack. He wouldn't ask again.

"I suppose not," he said, almost sad. "Even if you agreed, I could never trust you not to take a blade to my back. Not after today." He sighed heavily. "Not after this."

"Ago," she whispered, even her voice beginning to fail in its strength, "pugna quod int-"

"Quiet your tongue! This house is mine. Mine." He let go of her chin and her head drooped. "And you can die knowing that I have taken more than what you all refused to give me in life."

"A place at our table," Josselyn said, her tone softer still, the will to live leaving her. Her heart called out to her ancestors, to her dead family, begging them to come and get her.

"My table," he answered, stepping away. The General lifted a gun, pointing it at her head. She heard the telltale click of metal on metal. The weapon was not one found on the fifth moon. They fought with swords and axes, like the old medieval ways. Though technology was available, not using it was a point of honor. He must have brought the weapon from another moon. Perhaps the Victorians? The Elizabethans? It appeared to be too old to be from much later in time.

"Do it, Jack." She didn't look at him as she waited for the final discharge of the gun, the loud bang before the end. When it didn't come, she repeated, the words a mere mouthing of her lips, "Do it."

"Speed you to a quick end, Josselyn Craven," Jack whispered. "You all brought this on yourselves."

To find out more about Michelle's books visit www.MichellePillow.com

THE SAVAGE KING

BY MICHELLE M. PILLOW

Lords of the Var® Book One
A Qurilixen World Novel

Bestselling Cat-shifter Romance Series

Cat-shifting King Kirill knows he must do his duty by his people. When his father unexpectedly dies, it's his destiny to take the throne and all of the responsibility that entails. What he hadn't prepared for is the troublesome prisoner that's now his to deal with.

Undercover Agent Ulyssa is no man's captive. Trapped in a primitive forest awaiting pickup, she's going to make the best out of a bad situation… which doesn't include falling for the seductions of a king.

About *Lords of the Var*® (Books 1-5)

You met their father, King Attor, in Dragon Lords Books 1-4, now meet the Var Princes!

The cat-shifter princes were raised to not believe in love, especially love for one woman, and they will do everything in their power to live up to their father's expectations. Oh, how the mighty will fall.

The Savage King Excerpt

Kirill watched the door to his bedroom open. He'd been sitting in the dark, trying to relieve the stress headache that had built behind his eyes for the last week. The pain started at the base of his skull and radiated up to his temples until he could hardly see straight.

A heavy responsibility had been thrust on his shoulders, a responsibility he really hadn't prepared himself for, the welfare of the Var people. King Attor had not left him in a good position. He'd rallied the people to the brink of war, convinced them that the Draig were their enemy, and even went so far as to attack the Draig royal family.

Kirill wanted to see peace in the land. However, he knew the facts didn't bode well for it. The Draig had a long list of grievances against King Attor and the Var kingdom.

Before his death, the king had ordered an attack on the four Draig princes, all of which ended horribly for the Var. The worst was when Prince Yusef was stabbed in the back, a most cowardly embarrassment for the Var guard who did it. If he hadn't been executed in the Draig prisons, he would've been ostracized from the Var community. Luckily, Prince Yusef survived or they'd already be at battle.

Attor had also arranged for the kidnapping of Yusef's new bride. The Draig Princess Olena had been rescued, or that too would've led to war. The old king had even tried to poison Princess Morrigan, the future Draig queen, on two separate occasions. She too lived. And those were only a few of the offenses Kirill knew about in the few weeks before King Attor's death. He could just imagine what he didn't know.

Kirill sighed, feeling very tired. He'd known since birth that the day would come when he'd be expected to step up and lead the Var as their new king. He just hadn't expected it to be for another hundred or so years. His father had been a hard man, whom he'd foolishly believed was invincible.

"Here kitty, kitty, kitty." His lovely houseguest's whisper drew his complete attention from his heavy thoughts.

Ulyssa bent over like she expected him to answer to the insulting call. He dropped his fingers from his temple into his lap, and a quizzical smile came to his lips. As he watched her, he wasn't sure if he was angered or amused by her words.

"Are you in here, you little furball?" she said, a little louder.

She wore his clothes. Never had the outfit looked sexier. His jaw tightened in masculine interest, as he unabashedly looked her over. All too well did he remember the softness of her body against his and the gentle, offering pleasure of her sweet lips. She'd made soft whimpering noises when he'd touched her, yielding, purring sounds in the back of her throat. Even with the aid of nef, he was surprised by how easily and confidently she melted into him. The Var were wild, passionate people and were drawn to the same qualities in others. He suspected she'd be an untamed lover.

Too bad she'd belonged to his father first. In his mind, that made her completely untouchable though none would dare question his claim if he were to take her to his bed. Technically, by Var law, she belonged to him until he chose to release her. For an insane moment, he thought about keeping her as a lover. He knew he wouldn't, but the thought was entertaining.

Kirill's grin deepened. Ulyssa strode across his home to the bathroom door with an irritated scowl. It was obvious she didn't see him in the darkened corner, watching her. He detected her engaging smell from across the room, the smell of a woman's desire. It stirred his blood, making his limbs heavy with arousal. And, for the first time since his father's death, his headache relieved itself.

"Hum, maybe I'm looking too high. I'm sure there has to be a little cat door here somewhere. Come here, little kitty. Where are you hiding?"

His slight smile fell at her words. It was easy to detect her mocking tone.

"Where's your little kitty door, huh?" Ulyssa whispered to herself, her blue gaze searching around in the dark.

Kirill grimaced in further displeasure. He watched her open the door to his weapons cabinet. Her eyes rounded, and he thought she might take one. She didn't. Instead, she nodded in appreciation before closing the door and continuing her search for an exit.

She stopped at a narrow window by his kitchen doorway. Her neck craned to the side, as she tried to see out over the distance. Kirill knew she looked at the forest. From under her breath, he heard her vehement whisper, "Where exactly did you little fur balls bring me? Ugh, I need to get out of this flea trap, even if I have to fight every one of you cowardly felines to do it. I've fought species twice as big and three times as frightening. A couple of little kitty cats don't scare me."

If this insolent woman wanted to play tough, oh, he'd play. Curling gracefully forward, Kirill shifted before his hands even touched the ground. He let one thick paw land silently on the floor, followed by a second. Short black fur rippled over his tanned flesh, blending him into the shadows. His clothes fell from his body, and he lowered his head as he crept forward. A low sound of warning started in the back of his throat. He was livid.

**To find out more about Michelle's books
visit www.MichellePillow.com**

LOVE POTIONS

BY MICHELLE M. PILLOW

Warlocks MacGregor Book 1

Contemporary Paranormal Scottish Warlocks

A little magickal mischief never hurt anyone…

Erik MacGregor is from a clan of ancient Scottish warlocks. He isn't looking for love. After centuries, it's not even a consideration…until he moves in next door to Lydia Barratt. It's clear that the shy beauty wants nothing to do with him, but he's drawn to her and determined to win her over.

The last thing Lydia Barratt needs is a demanding Scottish man meddling in her private life. Just because he's gorgeous and totally rocks a kilt doesn't mean she's going to fall for his seductive manner.

But Erik won't give up and just as Lydia lets her

guard down, his sister decides to get involved. Her little love potion prank goes terribly wrong, making Lydia the target of his sudden embarrassingly obsessive behavior. They'll have to find a way to pull Erik out of the spell fast when it becomes clear that Lydia has more than a lovesick warlock to worry about.

Warning: Contains yummy, hot, mischievous MacGregors who may or may not be wielding love potion magick in an effort to prank their older brother, and who are almost certainly up to no good on their quest to find true love.

Love Potions Excerpt

"Ly-di-ah! I sit beneath your window, laaaass, singing 'cause I loooove your a——"

"For the love of St. Francis of Assisi, someone call a vet. There is an injured animal screaming in pain outside," Charlotte interrupted the flow of music in ill-humor.

Lydia lifted her forehead from the kitchen table. Her windows and doors were all locked, and yet Erik's endlessly verbose singing penetrated the barrier of glass and wood with ease.

Charlotte held her head and blinked heavily.

Her red-rimmed eyes were filled with the all too poignant look of a hangover. She took a seat at the table and laid her head down. Her moan sounded something like, "I'm never moving again."

"You need fluids," Lydia prescribed, getting up to pour unsweetened herbal tea from the pitcher in the fridge. She'd mixed it especially for her friend. It was Gramma Annabelle's hangover recipe of willow bark, peppermint, carrot, and ginger. The old lady always had a fresh supply of it in the house while she was alive. Apparently, being a natural witch also meant in partaking in natural liquors. Annabelle had kept a steady supply of moonshine stashed in the basement. If the concert didn't stop soon she might try to find an old bottle.

"*Ly-di-ah!*"

"Omigod. Kill me," Charlotte moaned. "No. Kill him. Then kill me."

"*Ly-di-ah!*"

Erik had been singing for over an hour. At first, he'd tried to come inside. She'd not invited him and the barrier spell sent him sprawling back into the yard. He didn't seem to mind as he found a seat on some landscaping timbers and began his serenade. The last time she'd asked him to be quiet, he'd gotten louder and overly enthusiastic. In fact, she'd been too scared to pull back the curtains for a clearer look, but she was pretty sure he'd been dancing on her lawn, shaking his kilt.

"Omigod," Charlotte muttered, pushing up and angrily going to a window. Then grimacing, she said, "Is he wearing a tux jacket with his kilt?"

"Don't let him see you," Lydia cried out in a panic. It was too late. The song began with renewed force.

"He's..." Charlotte frowned. "I think it's dancing."

Since the damage was done, Lydia joined Charlotte at the window. Erik grinned. He lifted his arms to the side and kicked his legs, bouncing around the yard like a kid on too much sugar. "Maybe it's a traditional Scottish dance?"

Both women tilted their heads in unison as his kilt kicked up to show his perfectly formed ass.

"He's not wearing..." Charlotte began.

"I know. He doesn't," Lydia answered. Damn, the man had a fine body. Too bad Malina's trick had turned him insane.

To find out more about Michelle's books visit www.MichellePillow.com